Cold As Hell

Neen Cohen

First Edition
Published by Breaking Rules Publishing Europe, 2021.
This is a work of fiction. Similarities to real people, places, or events are entirely coincidental.
Cold As Hell
9789198684056
Copyright © 2021 Neen Cohen.
Written by Neen Cohen

4

Cold as Hell could not have happened without the encouragement and patience of my partner, and our son. The friendship and support of Aiki Flinthart, Pamela Jeffs, and the Springfield Writers Group have also been instrumental in getting this story finished.

Prologue

"No more pushing books around that bloody library." Mikayla nodded, convinced she'd made the correct choice. "If I see you again, OpenFields, it'll be too soon. Maybe I'll head to Brisbane, it's only 200 miles away. Ha, *only*."

Long shards of light stretched across the town in pinks and oranges, fading into bruises of purple and black. The fingers of light pulled away as the sun slipped further behind the buildings and sank over the horizon.

As night claimed its time, Mikayla Smith took a deep breath and stepped over the boundary of the town and out into the big wide world. The sign that screamed in large red letters that she was leaving OpenFields and to come back soon wasn't the only indicator of this bold step. One moment her steps were cushioned against the soft carpet of moist and nutrient-rich grass, the next dead, dry crunching beneath the soles of her shoes.

Three steps and Mikayla paused. She closed her eyes, waiting. Liquid lightning continued to run beneath her skin, and she reached her mind out toward the surrounding earth. Brown blades swelled and softened around her black, thick-soled boots. The magic lingered there; she could feel it just as strongly as in town. She smiled and hope bloomed inside her chest.

"A few more steps?" Mikayla muttered to herself.

She had decided; she was saying goodbye to the magic to sate her wanderlust.

But the magic was supposed to end at the town's sign. It was what they had all been taught, what she had always known.

Green luscious grass cradled her steps, the magic fizzing out of her, feeding her surroundings, like static raising the hair on her body when she dragged her feet through the carpet in the town hall, the hub of all OpenFields activity.

She gasped as a shadow, tall and featureless, detached from the ragged shrubs at the side of the road.

"Hello?" Mikayla's voice cracked, her heart speeding beneath her chest.

The shadow moved toward her, smooth and soundless.

Her breath caught, her heart pumped faster, the magic raced to an aching pulse beneath her skin. She turned back toward the safety of her town. The spotless sign beckoned: Welcome to OpenFields.

Run!

The shadow's presence, black and sharp like metal on the back of her tongue, slowed her steps. Mikayla had never been in quicksand, but she had an inclination of what that might feel like. Beads of sweat collected on her forehead as she forced a step toward home and safety. With trembling legs and aching arms, she collapsed to the soft ground of promise inside the sign and boundaries of OpenFields.

Her breath swayed the green grass in front of her, and tears stung the corners of her eyes. The night noises of the town were drowned out by the roar of blood in her ears while her nose filled with the richness of wet dirt and summer heat.

Time was irrelevant. It had been ten minutes or two hours when Mikayla pushed herself to her feet. Spider legs of anxiety creeping up her spine. She turned around. She had to know. Using the edge of the town's sign to keep her throbbing legs from collapsing beneath her weight, she stared out past the town and its safety.

Mikayla saw nothing. No detached shadows or spikes of adrenaline raising the hairs on the back of her neck. If she could, she would have put it down to her overactive imagination, but she was born and bred in OpenFields, Mikayla wasn't delusional. She knew the touch of magic all too well.

With a small shake of her head, a shudder in her shoulders, and a small laugh that sounded like a scream in the still darkness, she turned around, back to her town.

The scream choked in her throat.

The shadow stood in front of her. Inside of OpenFields.

"No!" The word came out small and rough.

The black cowl that covered the head nodded slowly up and down.

Death? The Grim Reaper? He doesn't belong in OpenFields. He has no power here!

But the cowled figure stepped forward, the blades of grass parting to the pressure of his boots.

Not death.

Hands, pale and soft in the moonlight, reached toward Mikayla.

Run!

Before she could move a step, her legs gave way as coldness washed over her. It started in her hair and splashed down her neck. It froze the breath in her lungs and turned her stomach into sharp tipped icebergs. Life and colour drained from the surrounding grass, the blades turning brown as her fingers trembled and reached for them.

Not-Death stepped forward, and those fingers fluttered down and lifted Mikayla's chin until she was looking into the dark depths of the hood. Unshed tears pricked at her eyes as the hands cradled her head, palms warm against her skin.

The roar of blood screamed in her ears and Mikayla didn't notice the stillness of the world around her, the silencing of life.

With a strength the softness belied, the hands tightened and with a sharp jerk snapped Mikayla's neck.

***

The shadow watched, waiting until the body crumpled into pure stillness before scooping it up into powerful arms that shone pale beneath the shifting cloak.

Death had arrived in OpenFields

Chapter 1

Magic existed in OpenFields. And the magic was a drug. It was an ache in the jaw bones as though sugared syrup had been held in the mouth too long before it dripped acid sweetness down the back of the throat. Once a person tasted it, the craving was always inside of them, forgetting the sting and the ache and remembering only the rush. People did stupid things for their next hit.

Adie loved the town, the fresh air and the views from Dedication Rock, the familiarity, and the vibrations she felt in the centre of town. She loved it, even despite the people, the church, and the rush she craved and feared in equal measure, often simultaneously. Even when she stopped investigating, asking over and over about the magic, its source and the true name of their deity, the craving and the love had always been enough to keep her from leaving.

She scowled and gave the finger to the camera up in the room's corner, the one they used to watch her sleep. She shifted her gaze to the wall of books. They were piled up on top of each other, second-hand volumes pilfered wherever she could find them. The pages were filled with adventures of those braver than herself. She had wept promises to characters that meant more to her than any of the town's residents. Promises that one day she would find that strength to leave.

She wasn't sure what her current home had originally been used for, but she doubted it had been intended for someone to live in.

Perhaps an office.

The kitchenette was enough to make toast, brew a coffee, and heat microwavable dinners. The only closed off room was the bathroom and toilet in one.

Adie had painted the door to the bathroom: a field of bright yellow sunflowers. In the centre stood a gnarled chocolate-brown climbing tree, trunk thick and gnarled with a layer of leaves surrounding it. Autumn colours of green, gold, and red created a rainbow over the sea of sunshine below. Beside that and the books, nothing else personalised the space as her own. No photographs or artworks hanging on the wall, no knick-knacks to express her individuality.

Time ticked by and soon her alarm would sound in the high pitched shrill. The only noise that was guaranteed to get her out of bed.

Groaning, Adie pushed the blankets away and instantly regretted it. She grabbed the folded azure blue throw rug from the end of her bed and wrapped it around her shoulders, continuing to shiver beneath layers of blanket and nightmare sweat.

Always the same nightmare.

She scurried to the kitchen; her socked feet whooshing along the wooden floorboards. Adie flicked the kettle before shuffling to shut the window near the closed bathroom door.

Twelve steps, kettle to window. Counting. A distracter she had used ever since she could remember.

She reached to pull the window closed and was entranced by the tendrils of light reaching out over the horizon. The cold bit bone deep, but the colours so vibrant, pinks and oranges merged with purples and yellows, pushing away the darkness. Reminding her of the flames she never learnt to control.

They were bright against the bleak path her thoughts threatened to take. Adie scanned the horizon, smiling at each reaching flame, each tendril.

Along the horizon, her rainbow view was interrupted by a figure of darkness. Adie blinked; certain it must be nothing more than a trick of the light.

The figure remained, looming in the brilliant daylight, a new stain on the horizon.

No, it's a tree!

But she knew she was wrong. She stared at this view many times, daydreaming. There was no tree there, nothing except her imaginary adventures of walking past the horizon and leaving this town behind.

The figure lifted an arm, waved as though by the force of a strong wind. Adie's rose in response, a familiarity nudged at the edges of her thoughts. The sound of the kettle clicked, and Adie blinked. The figure vanished. Not slowly fading, but poof in that instant, a mere finger snap.

She shivered against more than the weather, pulling the window closed with a reluctant creak.

Wrapping the blanket tighter around her shoulders, she found the plastic bottle on her bedside table and took two of the small white bitter pills. Not that they had worked last night. The nightmare had returned louder than before. The magic buzzed beneath her skin; it had been the catalyst that finally woke her and pulled her from her nightmare.

Adie was glad it was Saturday, as working in the library in the centre of town while the buzzing continued beneath her skin would have been unbearable. She couldn't remember the center of town's magic crawling over her skin any stronger than anywhere else, but she had never been deaf to the conversations of the chosen ones, and their excitement of the town's energy. Even with Lisa's help—her cool touch was a balm on the bad days, the mornings after the nightmares. But today it felt different. Would she tell Lisa? Her stomach tumbled at the thought before Adie reminded herself that her friend was nothing like her mother.

But things were shifting, even Adie felt it. The last few months, a storm had steadily built around the town, the tense atmosphere simply waiting for the deluge to break through. Now it felt as though it was building inside of Adie as well.

Shivering again, Adie wished the pressure came with heat, or at least humidity.

15

"Well, gotta love bad omens on a morning that feels like the ice age is making a comeback," she mumbled to herself. Each morning had been colder than the last, and winter hadn't even officially started yet.

She made her cup of chai and sat at one of her mismatched chairs at the small round table in the corner. It was the scarred wooden one with the red cushion she tied to the seat—more comfortable than the straight backed one that wouldn't let her slouch, or the black metal chair with the slight bend in one leg that wobbled back and forth with the slightest movement. She sipped her brew, savouring the sweet milky spice with its hints of cinnamon. The warmth spread to her fingers, making them tingle.

She pushed the image of the waving shadow from her mind. She couldn't tell anyone about it, not even Lisa. She would only give the town another reason to ostracise her. Hallucinating would be another mark against the suicidal dark creature they tolerated but couldn't get rid of. This was her home, after all.

But it wasn't, really. It never had been.

She came here when she was six. And before that, there was nothing. No memories, no life.

Just a name. Adeline. Not even a good one.

But the magic had come so easily, drawn to her from the moment she could remember being in OpenFields. There was an electricity beneath her skin. An aural sensation that vibrated and created colours around all that she saw. A heat weaved through her, even before she was a conduit. People in town had told her how that was OpenFields gift;

16

how the magic that coursed through her veins was a gift from the goddess, one not shared anywhere else. She had accepted the town and embraced the learnings interweaved with standard school lessons.

The magic came from the earth, OpenFields being the sacred place where the bones of the first goddess were returned to her natural element. Those that were honoured and blessed for their dedication filled OpenFields. They maintained its beauty, and they never failed to remember her. Engraved images of the goddess adorned the town and the people.

Their Town Leader, Mr Kenjins, had direct correspondence to their deity. He communed with her in sacred rituals. In return, she offered him and her followers the essence of her power. The magic that ran through OpenFields' veins.

The goddess gave Mr Kenjins guidance and direction, and in return he would choose those most dedicated to becoming direct conduits of the magic. Only the strongest of her followers, those strong enough to contain it and share it with the other residents of the town. Each conduit's powers manifested differently when receiving the essence of the goddess, though all were rooted in the elements. Some fire conduits could ease the wrath of the flames, while others could only create a spark with no control over where it would burn. Adie loved to watch the earth conduits as they helped flowers bloom by guiding roots to the most nutrient-rich soil. There were also those who could manipulate water while others could create it, and while clouds could be summoned by almost all elements, not all conduits could force them to weep.

She had once asked why they couldn't stop the drought ravaging towns outside of OpenFields. After being scowled at, she was told the will of the earth was not theirs to question.

She had only been eight years old.

When Adie had become a conduit, aged sixteen, the darkness it brought out in her was unbearable. The power had flooded her, while flames danced on the tips of her fingers. She had laughed until it burnt within. It was beautiful until it became too strong, and she set things alight without control.

Her understanding and acceptance had been replaced with nightmares and fear.

Well, a nightmare. Just the one. Over and over again.

The cave was dark and veined with colours she couldn't quite catch or name. The open space around her was little more than a mirage, the trapped and foreboding feelings pressed against her chest. She sensed the tunnel behind her and knew there were no other means of escape.

In front of her the beast stood, dripping someone else's blood from fangs that pushed his top jaw over his chin. The eyes were wide open, burning flames within. Adie focused on the face. Its canine features: long snout, pointed ears and wide smiling mouth. But the body reminded her of a bull, muscular and powerful. Ragged bristly fur shuddered under his movements, his raging. But the stomping was nothing more than show. His back hooves were chained to the wall behind him, dried blood coating legs and cuffs alike. Sores and scabs half hidden beneath the shifting cuffs and his hair worn away, revealing dirty skin beneath.

Against the walls, figures carved from dark glistening rock surrounded him; all the faces warped unrecognisable except for their frozen silent screams. Glowing red pulsed inside the chest of each figure; a beating heart trapped by the slobbering beast, or crimson colours trapping the slobbering beast?

Adie drew closer, her body threatening to fall as her foot dropped lower, into the groove of the earth she hadn't seen. Squinting closer in the intermittent light, Adie realised that she now stood in an indent of the ground in the cave. The beast and the statues on the ledge of the other side.

The fear of the beast came and went as the image flickered, like an overlain celluloid strip of a movie reel.

One moment the beast snarled and pulled against the chains that had nothing to give. Then with a flick, a snap of unseen fingers, he became a man; malnourished and chained to the black rock wall by his wrists with chains thicker than his neck. His clothing was little more than strips of dirty decaying rags, the original colour hidden beneath age and grime. The colour of his skin, hair and eyes was unknowable in the dirt and gloom. But like beacons, raised white welts covered much of the skin that stretched too tightly over bone. Sitting beside the man was a stone lidless coffin, more terrifying than the beast and the man combined.

The image flicked back and forth, a voice begging for help while another screamed. She couldn't tell if it was the beast or man which howled for mercy.

The screaming and the begging bled together, mixed and grew louder until she staggered back; out of the cave, into the tunnel, and returned to the waking world.

Fingers slipped beneath Adie's wrist bands, fingers trailing over the raised flesh. Memories of her weakness. She never took the bands off, not even to shower. The sight always proved more than she could bear, even if her fingertips sought out their grooves when the nightmare grew too loud. Despite the discomfort her fingertips sought out these marks whenever the nightmares, or the waking world, felt too heavy. Adie didn't know if she reminded, or continued to punish, herself.

The tablets kept her safe. Kept her mind intact. Kept the fire inside, safe from hurting anyone. But the nightmare always returned worse than ever, and the fear coiled like a dark snake in the pit of her stomach, ready to strike with a tongue made of flames.

Adie waited for the kettle to boil for her second cuppa of the morning while she made toast. She slathered the near burnt piece of bread in butter then cut thick chunky slices of tomato.

She sliced the last piece of tomato, her stomach growling in anticipation of the salty tart combination. The unexpected knock on her front door made her jerk, the knife slipping into the fingerprint pads of three fingers on her left hand.

"Fuck."

The blood flowed too quickly, splashing over her breakfast, the crimson mixing with the red tomatoes, staining the wet bread. She raced to the sink, pouting at her ruined food. Her stomach churned, the hunger gone at the sight and smell of blood.

Adie looked toward the front door as the knock came again.

This was her sanctuary. Monitored or not, she was given relative freedom here and she savoured what little she had.

Guests weren't welcomed, she had never sent out invitations.

"Coming," Adie called out reluctantly as she rifled through the crap drawer in the kitchen for some sticking plasters.

Pulling the door open she stood for a moment wondering if she had woken up, or the dreams continued, twisting into a just as familiar real-life nightmare. Billie stood on the doorstep. It had been years since she had seen her old friend up close instead of from a distance, or in her dreams.

"What the hell are you doing here? And what the hell are you wearing?"

The last few years had been kind to Billie. Adie couldn't help but feel a little woe is me over this annoying fact. Where was karma now?

Where Adie's thighs and waist had thickened and her dark dense hair became wilder and more unmanageable no matter what she did, Billie had simply grown more barbie-like.

Of course, it would be Billie at the door. No one else would brave it.

They had been inseparable once upon a time.

Chapter 2

B illie was wrapped up in a pink oversized jacket, made from some kind of '80s vinyl, and a pair of jeans that looked like they had been buried in a box in the bottom of a cupboard for many years. Okay, so maybe karma had a better sense of humour than Adie expected.

Adie hadn't known if Billie even knew where she lived.

"Adie, something's happened in town."

"And?" Adie's anxiety was lightning beneath her skin, desperate to find some patch of ground to release to.

"Get dressed, everyone's being called to the great hall."

"Get fucked, Billie. I'm not running at your heels like a dog."

"Please, Adie?"

Please?

Adie bit her top lip.

"Please?" Bille asked again, eyes pleading.

Adie sighed. That look always worked. "Fine. Come in while I get dressed."

Billie shook her head and stepped back, away from the door's threshold. The left side of Adie's lip lifted, barely containing the growl building in her throat. Her eyes flicked to the camera as she closed the door again, flipping it the bird once more.

She wasn't sure who had to watch the footage, if it was recorded or not, but she used every chance she could to make sure all sets of eyes knew she understood how fucked up this was, and how much she didn't approve.

She walked to her cupboard, which was nothing more than a 16-cube china white bookshelf that served its life having clothes unceremoniously thrown into it.

Sometimes they were folded. *Sometimes.*

Adie jammed a shirt over her head and shoved her feet ruthlessly into sneakers. She pulled the laces too tightly and had to undo and try again. As she buttoned up her jeans, she shook her head. Facing the townspeople on the weekend was not her idea of a good time.

She scoffed as she straightened the hem of her shirt, pulling it more out of shape. There weren't any mirrors in the house, too dangerous a risk for her. The outfit would do, no matter how out of shape. Her tongue ran over her teeth. A calming habit that wasn't working.

What was she doing?

On a whim, Adie grabbed her work backpack and flung it on before walking to her front door. Its weight a comfort as it settled, the bottom pressing gently into the small of her back. Leaving right now, going to where she didn't want to be, seemed like such a final departure, although she couldn't imagine how. She pulled her door open and revelled at the sight of Billie shivering on the footpath at the front of her place.

Serves you right.

Billie hopped from foot to foot, hands rubbing at her arms through the thick puffy highlighter-pink jacket. If Adie didn't have the nervous electricity still running beneath her skin, and the residual memory of the nightmare, she could almost have burst out laughing.

She doubted anyone in the town had ever seen Billie in anything even remotely crumpled. Until now. The look should have given her more satisfaction, but she ached for the friendship they once had.

So she headed off to the town hall, her teeth biting deeply into her top lip. All it had taken was for Billie to say *please*. Adie doubted she would have as much power had the roles been reversed.

She locked the door, wondering why she bothered. The old weathered wooden door could probably have been blown in with the gentlest of breezes, and the lock snapped with a nudge from her hip.

Following a step or two behind Billie, Adie noticed that Billie's hair was unbrushed, pulled back into a chunky ponytail. Inconceivable. The town's perfect princess dishevelled?

"So, are you going to tell me what the hell is going on?"

Billie shook her head. Sunflower blonde locks bouncing along, flying left and right.

Adie stopped and turned around, heading back toward her home. "I'm not playing your games, Billie."

Billie grabbed Adie's arm. The sensation sent a warmth directly to Adie's cheeks. She clenched her teeth and looked pointedly down at Billie's long, slender fingers.

Billie released Adie's arm and mumbled an apology.

"Dad asked me not to say anything, just to get everyone to the town hall."

"So," Adie smiled. A grim one. "You drew the short straw in getting me. I'm still not going until you tell me what the hell is going on."

"Dr Simms."

"What about her?" Adie's words came out between clenched teeth.

The last time Adie had seen Dr Simms hadn't gone so well. Adie needed a new script and getting it from the good doc had felt somewhat akin to pulling teeth. Adie had yelled, while Dr Simms had remained perched nonchalantly on the edge of her desk, her slight frame hidden behind the starched white doctor's coat. Adie had yelled more. The doc's smile simply grew smug as the door opened and Sheryl, her secretary, barged in, all heroic and worried. Adie had to go two days without pills before the fresh bottle had been left in her letter box.

During those 48 hours, the electricity had returned in full force beneath her skin, much like this morning. Her blood had run like lava and the nightmares were walking hallucinations. So vivid, she had taken the rest of the week off work. She remembered all too clearly sitting in the corner of her room, screaming at the camera and the tree on the bathroom door that swayed in non-existent breezes, mocking her sanity.

The withdrawal from the magic, once she started on the tablets again, was almost as bad.

"Sheryl found her this morning when she went to open the surgery."

"Found her what? Spell it out, Billie." But the clenched fist in Adie's stomach, the thickness of her tongue, told her what she already knew.

"She's dead."

"How?" Adie pushed the word out through her suddenly dry mouth, the shadow she saw waving at her that morning blooming in her thoughts.

"It wasn't a natural death."

"Suicide?" The idea made Adie's breath quicken. A quick shake of Billie's head in the negative calmed Adie's breathing slightly. She should be more concerned about a murderer in OpenFields, but at least this way the good doc hadn't gotten the one thing she ... no!

Adie shook her head and focused on now.

"Then who?"

"No one seems to know."

The fist in Adie's stomach twisted. It felt like a creature had buried itself inside of her and was now eager to crawl back out.

"I have an alibi, Billie. You know that. *They* know that."

"You aren't a suspect."

"Then why am I being summoned?"

27

"Everyone's getting brought to the town hall. I don't know what else is happening, but I can feel it in the earth. Something's not right. Something more than Dr Simms' murder."

Murder.

The word brought a bubble of laughter up to Adie's throat.

It just didn't happen in OpenFields. The magic protected all of them. That was why they stayed, why they cared for the earth. It was symbiotic.

The image on the skyline, arm lifting as if in greeting, flashed across Adie's memory once more. She tried to mentally place an image of Dr Simms over the misty figure. The image was almost amusing. They definitely didn't match.

But something was wrong. Even on the tablets, Adie could feel it. Why could she feel it? She nodded and headed toward town.

3793 steps of silence before they both stood in front of the town hall. It featured a large clock tower that didn't even pretend to be anything but a phallic symbol, with a front facade of large rough-hewn stone. It was weathered and grey no matter how many times they used the gurney on it and stood out against the more modern designs of the surrounding town. Which made sense. The town had sprung up around the hall according to the histories, and Adie had never found any reason to doubt them.

The hall looked across the road to the town square, where the mumbling of almost four hundred people was a

28

buzz against their ears. It was all but filled, the green overtaken by a mix of dark and too bright clothing.

"I thought you said we were meeting in the hall?"

"We were."

"Has anyone spoken to Lisa?"

Billie's eyes narrowed at Adie before leaving her and making a beeline toward her father. Mr Kenjins, Town Leader, tall and lean with large strong hands and a crooked nose that always made Adie wonder how he broke it. Far too many times, she had imagined incrementally more hideous events—a clenched fist from the first girl he asked out, a horse's hoof to the face, a trip over his cocky arrogance in front of the entire town—and wishing she had footage. He stood up on the small gazebo, talking to someone whose back was to Adie. She couldn't tell who it was. She was certain the person was female, but it wasn't a woman from the town. The haircut was too short. If someone had decided on such a dramatic change, it would easily have been big news.

Even Adie would have heard about it.

She scanned the crowd. Everyone's arms were waving and mouths flapping. Adie saw no sign of Lisa.

The town green square was Adie's favourite place to be. The grass and earth were grounding. She would sit during her lunch breaks from the library and take off her shoes, feel the power in the earth she no longer felt vibrating beneath her skin every waking moment.

It calmed and terrified.

29

She loved watching as others focused on different plants and trees and had them bend to their will. It was addictive in its pain. Like worrying a sore tooth with your tongue. The pain of not being able to touch the magic was worth seeing it.

It was better than being cut off completely.

In the town square no one hid it from her, as though she weren't unworthy of its touch.

She knew she was.

The centre of town was little more than a main street with houses surrounding it like a barrier from the outside world. The town had only one of everything. A bookshop, a hairdresser, and a laundromat lined up like a pub joke on the right-hand side of the town hall. To the left were the library, the post office, and the pub itself. The public toilets were set slightly back and next to them were the clothing store, the doctors' surgery, the shoe shop, and the bakery. The rest of that side of the street was filled with the town's grocery store. Adie could walk from the roundabout near the bookshop all the way to the end of the grocery store in little more than ten minutes. 1392 steps.

1000 steps exactly to the start of the doctor's surgery.

With a start, Adie remembered why everyone was there.

The town square would never be the same again. It was taken over by the murder of the doctor. Murder. In OpenFields! The very idea would have been laughable if not for the scrunched eyebrows on every face she saw. Tears streaking through makeup on women's faces who had never

30

let their own husbands see them less than perfect. Protective arms wrapped around children, hands gripping shoulders to pull them closer than comfortable.

Then nausea roiled in Adie's belly as she noticed the light in every third or fourth set of eyes. There was an excited buzz, like a swarm of wasps emanating from the crowd. A woman had been murdered by someone in their own town, and all they could think about was the excitement of something new and different. It was as obvious as though they had speech bubbles over their heads.

Adie shook her head. She couldn't look at any of them anymore, the scared or the excited. She finally tuned in to what Mr Kenjins was saying.

And froze as she stared at the woman who had turned around and looked out over the crowd. A stranger yes, but the familiarity was an itch at the back of Adie's mind. She couldn't have been much older than Adie, a year or two if that. A sharp chin, big eyes, and skin so smooth Adie's finger itched to stroke it.

Adie crossed the road, not bothering to check left or right. Almost everyone in town stood in front of her. Who would be driving past to hit her? The woman's eyes met Adie's as she stepped on to the grass and Adie's stomach clenched and did a small flip.

What was that about?

The smallest of nods before the woman's eyes drifted over the crowd again. They were familiar in a way that was impossible. Adie knew she had never seen this woman before in her life.

"I have promised Detective Tala that everyone in town will willingly and happily answer her questions and assist in anything she and her team need. They will stay at The Inn."

Detective? Staying?

There was no way she was old enough to be a detective. And *staying*? No one stayed in their town except during the Celebration of Flowers. It was the only reason the Inn was even built, and the celebration was months away. Hiding their magic in plain sight had kept the town from being looked at too closely.

Except for that one reporter.

"There will be a memorial for Dr Simms this afternoon."

Adie's eyes met Detective Tala's again, before she turned and walked away from the crowd, heading toward the library.

48 steps.

Adie looked back over her shoulder. The townspeople were all mesmerised by Mr Kenjins and Detective Tala. For a moment, Adie forgot what she was doing, caught up with the strange sensation that danced beneath her skin when she looked at the detective.

Shaking her head, Adie pulled her access card from her backpack and slipped into the library.

"Lisa?" Adie opened Lisa's office and stood blinking in the threshold. The office was never this messy.

Papers littered Lisa's desk, her pristine piles tipped and flowing on to the floor. Her drawers stood open and the chair Adie usually sat on during staff meetings was on its side. She stepped over the threshold and collapsed to her knees, looking closer at the mess.

"What the hell is going on?" Adie's voice echoed around the dishevelled office.

"That's what I'm here to find out." The voice was a low rumble that sent Adie's heart pulsing against pressure, as though a too-small rubber band had slipped around her chest.

She turned and stared, wide eyed, as the detective pulled on some cream-coloured latex gloves.

"Have you touched anything?"

Adie shook her head and watched as the woman walked around the room, commanding the very air to pay attention to her presence. She touched nothing, even with the gloves on, but leant close to a book that was open on the windowsill behind Lisa's desk.

"Why did you come here?"

It took a few moments for Adie to realise an answer was expected from her.

"I didn't see Lisa in the crowd. She's my boss, and Dr Simms' daughter. I just wanted to check she was okay."

"So, you work here?"

"Yeah. The last few years."

"Who else does?"

"I think she has some casuals on the books. I rarely see them; they work weekends mostly. The turnover's pretty high, usually just town kids waiting for something better to come along, usually out of town."

Adie hadn't realised how proud she was to be the only long-term employee of Lisa's. The only person who had stuck around for longer than just a few months. There were some that barely lasted a few weeks.

And yet every time Lisa mentioned another one had left - Mrs Jones' middle boy, or Mr Peters' youngest girl - envy would curl around Adie's chest.

"How many of you are there? Detectives, I mean," Adie asked.

"Just me for now. The rest are on their way."

"What about your partner, Detective Tala?"

Detective Tala's head snapped up from looking in the open drawers and glared at Adie. She could have sworn there was movement in Detective Tala's eyes. A skittering away. No, it was the dance of a flame. Adie had stared into fire enough times to know the pattern. Before the pills.

Adie faltered. "I... I just mean, don't you guys always go in twos?"

"Ah, he had car troubles. Should be here soon."

It was the first time Adie saw Detective Tala smile. It lit up her face, and Adie was reminded of a movie star she couldn't remember the name of.

"Detective Tala?"

"Just Tala."

"Oh," Adie blinked, struggling to remember the question that had just been on the tip of her tongue. "Okay, Tala? What happened to Doctor Simms?"

"What do you think happened?"

"I have no idea. I just got told that she died, and it wasn't natural."

"Who told you that?"

"Well, don't you kind of confirm it just by being here?"

Adie didn't know why she felt the need to protect Billie. It wasn't like they were close anymore, all of that had changed years ago. But here she was diverting any dirt from flicking up on to her old friend, as though what Adie did still mattered.

That smile again made Adie forget Billie and focus on Tala, and only Tala. Images of what Tala might look like with far fewer clothes on. Legs, not long but eye-drawing as the shapely curves couldn't hide behind the dress pants nor could the flat stomach under the white shirt that, in the right light, hinted at sun kissed skin beneath. But for all that, Adie kept being drawn back to her face. It would have blended in among the rich and famous that smiled out from glossy-covered magazines.

The woman was gorgeous.

Adie's stomach flipped a few more times. She hadn't noticed in the distance and in the gazebo's shade, the touch of red that streaked through Tala's hair. Adie imagined it being described as strawberry blonde, but it reminded her of the bark of her favourite tree trunk. The one in the village green she would tuck herself up against, back moulding to the comforting coolness of the trunk, and read until she felt calm enough to spend another day in OpenFields, in this life.

If that's really what it was. At best, it felt nothing more than a half-life; surviving, trying to convince herself the hope of being connected once again was worth the not-living.

"I guess so." Tala smiled, glancing at Adie.

"So, are you able to tell me?"

"We aren't completely sure yet. There was a lot of blood."

The word made Adie grateful she never ended up eating. Her crimson-covered tomato toast still sitting on her bench at home, untouched.

"Where would Lisa be, seeing as she's obviously not here?" Tala asked, commanding her attention again.

"I don't know her that well." Adie was terrible at lying, and the raise of Tala's left eyebrow told her as much.

"Educated guess?"

"She lives down behind the green. Close to the overhang of Dedo Rock, near the old gold mining tunnels."

"Wanna show me?"

Like a fish out of water, Adie's mouth flapped around, looking for a viable way to say no. But she knew it wouldn't be worth being dragged in front of the town council if Tala mentioned her lack of assistance.

She wasn't a good liar, but she was good at bottling up the anger. Her life was controlled by this town, by the Town Leaders, and she felt betrayed and hard done by. She wasn't even born to this magic, but somehow being dragged here so young it had leaked beneath her skin and taken control. And nothing had been right since. Her right fingers slipped beneath the sweatband on her left wrist, grazing over the raised lines, like braille only she could read.

Adie pulled out a bottle from her pocket and dry swallowed two of the small bitter pills before nodding and heading out of Lisa's office.

While they were in the library, the town meeting had finished, although small clumps of people continued to natter. She felt all eyes on her, but no one dared speak until Adie and Tala had moved beyond hearing range.

It disturbed Adie, the excitement that continued to radiate off too many of them.

"So, is it just me or are some of your fellow townspeople nodding like I've already got the culprit?" Tala asked with a small V forming between her brows.

"It's not just you." That left eyebrow rose again. "I don't exactly fit in."

"I'm not sure that's a bad thing."

Adie smiled. Out of the corner of her eye, she took in this stranger walking beside her. Tala had only been in town mere moments and had seen beyond the perfect image of this town. The smile faltered. Adie didn't want the warmth that spread through her chest. She liked it too much, and soon Tala would leave and take the warmth with her. But the smile returned. It had been so long since she had been seen, even if it was incidental to Tala's concerning insight of the town.

Chapter 3

The air felt sucked out of Adie's body as she stepped up to Lisa's front door. The house was a modern marvel and stood out like a sore thumb surrounded by old weatherboard Queenslanders.

The door stood open, and the tang of Adie's nightmare, stinging her nostrils and making her stomach churn, floated out from the house.

"Stay behind me." Tala's voice was rougher, and her arm pushed Adie back as though she weighed little more than the breeze.

In the back of Adie's mind, she wondered why Tala didn't pull out her gun, but she was too occupied with the smell permeating from the house that tried to suffocate her. She wasn't even sure Tala had a gun. She hadn't noticed one. And why would she carry one? But she looked so much like the detectives in the shows she recorded all week and would binge watch on the weekends.

Adie flicked through a stack of insults she had lived with, about her lack of life and too much time watching crime series. It was true, and she enjoyed watching them, but the sneer behind the words drilled holes in her armour.

She shook her head, but the thoughts were replaced with images of Lisa, with her shoulder length platinum blonde hair that Adie loved running her fingers through. She had even plaited it one night when they lay in bed, the room smelling of sweat and sex, while Lisa talked about the latest books she had ordered for the library. Lisa was the one who had gotten Adie interested in those crime shows and obsessed with reading true crime books. But people didn't know that. They didn't know anything about the two of them outside of them being work colleagues.

Adie forced out a breath and focused on the dark blackish spill that blocked out a fair chunk of the cream plush carpet of Lisa's living room. The small red-turned-brown wine stain from one of Adie's fumbles was now gone. Her guilt, now hidden beneath a large tacky looking rug, was irrelevant beneath the horror of not knowing what had happened to Lisa, of losing Lisa. Even a secret friendship was better than having no one.

"Lisa?" Adie called, voice wavering and all too shrill.

The look Tala flashed at Adie made her extremely grateful the woman didn't have a gun drawn. She bit her top lip, her hands shaking and her legs moving automatically in follow-the-leader mode.

The house wasn't big. Two bedrooms, a kitchen, the living room, and a bathroom she had often joked about swinging a cat in.

It felt as though lifetimes passed as she quietly followed Tala's search. All cupboards and doors peered behind, and beds looked beneath.

"She's not here." Tala's shoulders dropped slightly.

"Is she, I— Is she dead?"

"Blood spreads a long way," Tala rested warm fingers on Adie's cheek. She tried to hide the shiver that ran across the back of her shoulder. She shouldn't be having thoughts like this about another woman, especially in Lisa's living room while Lisa was bleeding and missing. "There's no telling just how much is there, but from my educated guess, she was alive when she left here."

Adie hadn't expected Tala to be so open. Perhaps she really had seen too many cop shows.

"So where to from here?" She needed to find Lisa. They might not have been much more than friends with benefits, and even that term might have been a bit strong, but she was the closest person to a friend Adie had in the entire town.

And her guilt at being attracted to Tala made her desire to take up the search for Lisa that much stronger.

"She was your boss, right?"

"Yeah."

"Just your boss?"

Adie froze, staring at the detective. "Meaning?"

Tala simply raised that damned left eyebrow and looked at Adie with the patience of one who could wait for days.

"We were friends, we slept together a few times. That's not common knowledge."

Tala nodded, and Adie could have sworn there were traces of a smile at the edge of her full dark lips. "So?" Adie asked.

"What do you know about this town?" Tala asked. Adie blinked, not understanding how the conversation had taken a different turn.

"I've been here since I was six. It's an old school town that focuses on the old ways." The words tumbled out without thought or feeling. They all knew the words. They learnt them for situations just like this. Well, perhaps not exactly like this. Situations involving outsiders, which no one expected to have to deal with outside of the Celebration of Flowers.

"And the cult?"

Adie hadn't expected that, her face unable to hide her shock quickly enough. Tala pulled out a folded piece of newspaper from her pocket and handed it to Adie with a small flick of her wrist, the paper half opening by the time Adie took it.

She knew the article well enough.

Behind the glass on the bulletin board in the town hall, the article stood in prime position, and had been for the last seven months. Adie looked at it, instantly realising that the

41

one she had seen in the town hall was far smaller than the one she now held in her hands.

At the top of the article there were two pictures: one of Mr Kenjins, black and white but Adie was certain the man had makeup on, and beside him a light-haired beauty with a familiar sharp long face and eyelashes to die for. Adie already knew she was the interviewer. Around her neck was a thick chain-link necklace with a pendant shaped like a wolf's head. The eyes looked as though they were jewels or gems.

Adie scoffed under her breath as she reread words she already knew.

OpenFields Town Leader, Samuel Jenkins, chuckled as he responded to this reporter's questions about rumours of the town shunning those who weren't members of the 'religion'.

"No, not at all. We honour and respect the earth and in return we are rewarded with the beauty and perfection of our town. We are happy to share it with whoever wishes to live here, as long as they respect what we have created."

This was all that was behind the glass in the town hall. Locked away as though someone might deface the picture of 'Mr Samuel Jenkins' if it weren't. Such a simple name, one no-one in the town ever used. Not even the other adults, at least, not in Adie's presence. Adie had indeed imagined drawing many things on the man over the last few months. Now she read on:

But there have been many questionable actions from OpenFields, including their unwillingness to open their books of the town's residents and meeting notes. OpenFields has been referred to as a cult on more than one occasion, and there is nothing this reporter has seen to deny these allegations.

Adie bit back the laugh that wanted to escape. She wasn't entirely sure what she was finding so funny. Her eyes must have given something away, because Tala quickly took the newspaper from her loose grip, tucked it in her back pocket and guided Adie back out on to the street.

Adie enjoyed the feeling of Tala's warmth through her thick, deep green jacket. The giggles gained momentum at the thought.

She really needed to get laid.

Tala helped Adie over to the footpath at the front of Lisa's home. Adie's legs crumpled beneath her, Tala quickly guiding her to sit on the curb, her feet splayed out into the bitumen road.

"Put your head down and when you can, have some of this." Tala placed an open bottle of water on the edge of the curb next to Adie.

Moments passed and eventually Adie pulled out the small bottle from her pants pocket, shook it before tucking it away again, wishing she could risk just taking a few more. She'd already taken too many this morning. Not that they seemed to work much.

Instead, she first took small sips of water, and then big gulps, from the bottle. Five gulps. She completely drained it, not having realised she was even thirsty.

"What are the pills for?"

43

Tala and her questions.

"Anxiety." It was as close to the truth as she could get.

"So, what did you do to your fingers?"

Adie's felt her eyebrows pull together. *Her fingers?* Then realisation dawned.

"Oh, I sliced them instead of a tomato when I was making breakfast this morning."

Tala only nodded, and Adie felt an intense desire to justify herself. "I didn't even get to eat it. It's still sitting on my bench at home covered in blood."

The last word sat uncomfortably on the tip of her tongue and was her undoing.

Adie leaned forward and retched out half of the water bottle, regretting her eagerness to scull the whole thing.

"So, you're a resident of the town. Did you meet Diana Tracey?" Tala asked, as if Adie hadn't just vomited all over the curb.

"Who?"

"The reporter."

"Oh." Adie couldn't figure out the expression that flitted across Tala's face like a cloud racing across the sun. "No. I don't think anyone else did, except Mr Kenjins. And I'm not sure anyone would technically consider me a member of this town anymore."

The car pulled slowly around the corner into Lisa's street and drove toward them. Adie felt the air ripple, a memory from when the town's magic danced hot beneath her skin, as Tala tensed and pushed her shoulders back.

This was not the time for the tablets to stop working. Why weren't they working?

Adie's heart raced too quickly, and she felt that liquid fire beneath her skin, the one that led to the dark places of her anxiety.

The screaming and the begging bled together, mixed and grew louder.

"A walk will help settle you down a bit," Tala murmured.

Adie flicked her eyes from the car and back to Tala. She had to trust her instincts, and right now she knew she didn't want the car to find her there. She enjoyed being around Tala, too much maybe, even if Adie was certain the woman was lying about something.

And she was a stranger.

She nodded and let Tala help her get to her feet. Despite her slim appearance, Tala pulled Adie upright as though she weighed nothing more than an abandoned feather she had picked up from the grass.

They strolled down the street, away from the car.

"Hey ladies." The vehicle was beside them too quickly. Adie wasn't good at lying, but the vice grip Tala had on her arm made her know she had to at least try.

"Hi! Are you lost?" Adie tapped into that old school charm she had been taught for the Carnival of Flowers.

"Are we that obvious?" He had a chiselled jaw and Adie bit her top lip, holding back a laugh as she imagined him cast in a B-grade FBI movie. His partner had flicked a glance their way before turning ahead again, hands still at ten and two as though the car weren't stationary.

"Maybe a little. Everyone in the town knows each other. It's not hard to notice out of towners." She laughed, hoping the hysteria didn't reach their ears.

"So, both you ladies are from town?" He looked a little closer at Tala and her dark power suit. Adie would need to get her out of those clothes as soon as possible.

Don't think about getting her undressed.

"Yeah." Tala snarled in Adie's silence.

"And were you just at Lisa Simms' house?" The interrogation in his voice wasn't hidden behind his smile.

"Oh." Adie looked back over her shoulder toward Lisa's house, dried blood hiding secrets she was determined to find answers to. "I'm not sure. I was feeling sick, so we sat down for a little bit while my head cleared. I didn't really pay attention to where we were."

"Are you okay now?" His smile couldn't hide his disinterest in her answer.

Adie nodded and tried a small smile. The less she spoke, the better.

"Thanks, ladies. We'll see you again soon." There was no hope or question in his voice.

"No doubt, Officer." Tala's gravelled voice made the officer blink, as though a camera with an unexpected flash had just gone off in front of him.

"That's obvious too, huh?" He had kind eyes, despite the attempt at an interrogation, and smiled along with Adie's nervous laugh.

46

The car turned around in the next driveway and headed back to Lisa's. Adie and Tala continued to walk away in silence until they were three blocks away.

"You aren't a cop, are you?" Adie didn't really need to ask, she already knew. Had always known, whether she realised it or not.

"Am I that obvious?" Tala mimicked the square jawed officer from the car.

"Who are you and why are you here?"

"My name is Tala, that much is true. I'm here looking for Diana."

Chapter 4:

Diana? So, you mean the reporter is missing as well?" Adie's eyes narrowed as she stopped walking. "Why would you come here?"

Tala blinked at Adie, looking as though for a moment she hadn't remembered Adie was there at all.

"She came back to do a follow-up piece." Tala's rough voice was softer, her eyes looking everywhere but at Adie. "We lost contact with her a few days ago."

Adie chewed on her top lip, thinking through the information as she began walking toward the outskirts north of the town. No one had come to town; Diana had never shown up.

Adie's rundown and monitored abode was on the outskirts, south of the town. It was so close to the only entrance and exit of OpenFields that Adie rarely missed any visitors.

So why was Adie's stomach doing belly flops again?

"You love her?" Adie felt sick asking. Felt heat rush through her limbs as she knew the answer before Tala opened her mouth.

"Yes!"

"Are they the real cops? Here to investigate Dr Simms's murder?" The word tasted like the copper smell from Lisa's living room.

"I guess the flat tyre I gave them didn't hold them up nearly as long as I had hoped." Tala smiled over at Adie, their strides keeping pace with each other. Her wicked grin sent a laughing rumble of thunder to escape Adie's mouth. A shiver ran beneath Adie's skin, centering in her lower stomach.

What was wrong with her? Now was not the time to be thinking about sex.

"Why don't you want the cops looking for her?"

Tala looked closer. The V between her brows deepened as her eyes lingered on Adie. She felt as though her whole soul was being scanned. She imagined Tala exploring her body with her hands and mouth instead.

How can I be thinking about these things right now?

"They'll just get hurt. They don't know what they are dealing with."

How did I ever think this woman was a cop? How had she fooled Mr Kenjins?

Adie could feel the threat in Tala's words. It shivered through her, as her fingers played with the small bottle in the front pocket of her shorts.

"What are your plans?" Adie knew she should just turn around, stop walking and head back to Lisa's to help the real authorities, but she agreed with Tala's logic.

Adie wondered if Tala wasn't also in over her head.

"I have no idea, honestly." Tala's smile was raw.

It radiated through Adie and she felt drawn to help. This woman, whose eyes looked as though Adie might never get out if she were to get lost in them, needed her.

For the first time, someone needed her.

"Alright, then it's time for Dedo." Adie nodded. She had a course of action. It wasn't much, but it was something.

"Sorry?" Both of Tala's eyebrows raised as she flicked the look over at Adie.

"We'll go up to Dedo Rock. It's the only place you can think in this town. We can figure out all this shit, or at least figure out our next step."

"Our?"

"Yep. The way I see it, we're both missing someone, so why not look together?"

"You are very sure of yourself." Tala slowly smiled, her mouth reminding Adie of a flower opening.

Adie had never been less sure of herself, but she nodded and turned right down James Road toward the entrance to Dedo Rock.

It wasn't a huge lightning bolt thought that made her think of the plan. They were barely five minutes' walk from Dedo Rock. And she hadn't lied.

Up there, she didn't feel caged.

798 steps later they stopped at the unmarked entrance, a low hanging chain swaying across the start of the dirt track. Tala looked at Adie, all traces of a smile gone. Adie laughed and ducked beneath the chain, holding it up to let Tala follow her.

The chain had never stopped anyone, it would be unlatched by the time the sun went down.

"It's make-out central up here, but it's usually empty during the day. It's only interesting to Fielders when the sun goes down."

Adie took the lead. She could hear the gentle, soft tread of Tala behind her.

"Aren't you a Fielder?"

Adie shrugged, glad the heat in her cheeks couldn't be seen by Tala. She was unsure how to answer the question.

She was a Fielder. The denial made her feel sick. Her skin prickled.

Who was she if she wasn't a Fielder?

Tala wasn't a cop. That was a relief. But she was still an outsider. So why did Adie trust her more than anyone back in the town?

Adie shook her head slightly; words fought each other and tied her tongue. Was she confusing someone to trust with someone she just wanted to sleep with? It had been a while.

It was cool in the shade of the overhanging trees. Leaves brushed their tips over the dirt track. As they continued to walk up the sloping incline, the coolness of the town lost its edge, and soon Adie regretted her thick dark green jacket.

51

Mulch made of dying leaves layered the ground in front of them just before they reached the open area of the rock.

"This is gorgeous." Tala's voice was almost gentle.

Adie smiled in response to Tala's awe. It had always offered her so much more than a place to 'go parking.'

They looked out over the town and Adie felt her body ache with the sight. The streets were laid out in front of her in a pattern that had meant nothing before, but now they filled her with dread. The air vibrated black and heavy, a line that overlapped and ignored all the roads leading to where it grew too dark and blotted out the main street of the town. The black path grew out of the dark ball over the town and led to the field out the back of her home. She had never seen it before, not like this. Even before the tablets, when she was a good little conduit, the shimmer from up here was a light that glittered like oil on the road after rainfall. After a quick glance to see Tala looking nonplussed, Adie closed her eyes, counted to ten and opened them again. The darkness in the air remained.

Soon her breath was coming too quickly, too shallow, and she sat heavily near the edge of the overhanging rock.

"Are you okay?" Tala asked, her voice urgent.

"Something's wrong with the town. It might not look like much to you, but there is something sinister hovering over it." Tala's eyes flicked to the view and back to Adie, the V a dark red between her eyes. "It's a blackness, a dark rain cloud that is blocking the view, and it's poisoning my town."

"Do you know what it is?" Tala's familiar eyes looked hungry enough to consume Adie. She shook her head.

52

Where had she seen those eyes before?

"I don't know what it is, but I know it makes me feel like I'm suffocating, and the culprit is a snake inside my stomach slithering its way up my throat. Two people are missing and now a murder. Something isn't right."

"I can't go back into town, not until I know what's going on with the real cops. I only have so much control."

"Control?" Adie closed her eyes, her face crumpling at her own stupidity. What was Tala talking about?

"Nothing important."

"I'll go back in." Adie's stomach growled. "And grab some food while I suss out what's happening. Can I leave this here?"

"We'll both still be here when you get back." Tala tucked Adie's backpack protectively under her arm, like a duck with a baby chick.

"Okay, just head to the woods if anyone else shows up."

"Thanks." Tala smiled and Adie walked away before she opened her mouth and said something she couldn't take back, or worse...opened her mouth and said *nothing*.

The air was crisp and chilled as she got back into town, the air inside the circle of houses surrounding the main street heavy and cold. She took a deep breath in, forcing her mind to calm as the fresh air enveloped her. She shivered as she stepped within a stone's throw of the Town Hall.

Not a bad idea, throwing stones.

"Oh, Adeline dear, it's so good to see you." Adie stiffened as she breathed out. The nasal voice she never wanted to hear again assaulted her ears.

53

Adie stopped and stared at Mr Kenjins. Billie stood beside her father, staring down at her feet.

"Hello, Mr Kenjins." Adie nodded. "Belinda, lovely to see you."

"And you, Adeline." Billie barely flicked a glance up, eyes not meeting Adie's.

"I'm so glad you decided to come pay tribute to Dr Simms. She would have been glad to see you here."

Ah, shit! The memorial service. Definitely something she should have remembered.

The chips would have to wait. She hoped Tala would as well.

Adie forced a tight smile across her face.

"Shall we go in, girls?"

Adie nodded, smile still plastered in place and lightly put her hand through Mr Kenjins' offered elbow, trying to touch as little of him as she could. She had never liked the man, hated him since that night. And now the sinister air around him was almost visible.

Billie clung to her father's other arm.

Adie let herself be dragged through the front door of the town hall. She had relied on Dr Simms, but the woman had been no more than a dealer. When the darkness had gotten too much, Dr Simms had been the one to force those first tablets into her.

The walls of the town hall closed around Adie.

They walked through the carpeted hallway, past the bulletin board behind its glass. Adie forced her eyes not to linger on the half article.

The town meetings were held in the large auditorium inside the town hall. All important events for OpenFields were held there. Adie's feet followed the familiar path, making her cringe at the memories she tried to convince herself had been washed away.

Her body trembled beneath her skin and she felt the roiling nausea in her stomach warn her from speaking.

Once inside, Mr Kenjins was quickly pulled away for muttered discussions with fellow Town Leaders. Adie didn't miss the unsure look he threw her before he allowed himself to be caught up in the town's affairs.

The great hall was filled with pews lined up to face the large stage and podium. From the books she had read, it looked much like any other chapel she had seen. Some were far more elaborate in their stained-glass windows, but still, pretty much the same.

All except for the hundreds of candles that lit the room.

Flames danced shadows and light over the chattering congregation, and Adie wanted to scream as the flames called to her.

She shouldn't be hearing any calls, not with the pills she'd popped.

Adie barely had thirty seconds to get worked up, before Billie came to direct her to one of the pews where the unallocated sat. Those residents who were not conduits of the magic and this meeting would not be the receivers of it either. The unallocated might as well be lepers. She barely acknowledged Billie, but followed behind, ensuring not even their clothes brushed.

The ceremony started with a tribute to Dr Simms. She could sit through this nice and quiet, it shouldn't take too long, and then she would get back to Tala and figure out the mysteries that had plagued her since she came to this town.

One of those mysteries was Tala herself.

Adie forced her shoulders to relax. Deep breaths, counting each inhale and exhale. A calm washed over her. There was something about Tala that she needed to figure out.

But the calm didn't last, and the thoughts writhed away, too slippery to grasp.

As Adie predicted, the tribute didn't take long. But then, without warning, a town meeting began.

Right now, OpenFields appeared to be just like any other place Adie had read about. *Any other cult,* Adie silently scoffed to herself.

She had looked up all the religions she could in the library. They all seemed to contain a list of dos and don'ts. As far as Adie could tell, they were just as screwed up as OpenFields, in their own unique ways.

Lisa had originally gotten her interested in looking up religions. She loved to point out the beauty of ancient beliefs in rare books she got into the library.

The thought of Lisa made Adie's leg jiggle up and down.

Mr Kenjins held court, and the mooning calf eyes of the townspeople surrounding Adie made her stomach churn again. She had never been convinced of his greatness, of him being the only reason this town thrived.

But they all looked at him the same way, the unallocated worse of all. They lived in hope of being gifted by his words. They would do anything to be chosen, conduit or recipient, all drug addicts begging for a drop of the poison that every fibre of their being thrived for.

Despite her desire to stay detached, Adie was pulled to the faces of the conduits. They were easy to pick out. Heat built up inside her, as though she had walked into a kitchen with all its windows closed and the oven up as high a temperature as possible. Her breath became a pant as her insides felt placed in that imaginary oven; cooking, burning. And she saw her own haunted expression mirrored in the conduits' eyes. Faces unsmiling; teeth clenched and eyes desperate to be anywhere else in the world.

Once the mundane notices and announcements were done, the real meeting would begin, and they would make her leave. Her legs jiggled. She wanted to get out. She had to get out.

The front doors locked with no one going near, and the bulk of the attendees split into groups of conduits and recipients. It was a subtle move and shuffle. But the gap was definitive.

She had no way of getting out. Her jiggling legs grew faster and faster. She could feel the tightness gripping the back of her neck like a large meaty fist.

If she stood, if she tried to leave, she would bring the attention she had to avoid.

She remained seated, not sure her legs would have taken her weight had she been brave enough to stand.

Mr Kenjins' nasal voice began. Words no one understood, but everyone felt.

The words pulled Adie's organs around inside of her, like the witches mixing the pot in *Macbeth*. Mr Kenjins finished the first repetition, nodded, and lifted his arms. All conduits stood, legs slightly bent, grounding themselves for the purge.

As Mr Kenjins began the second recital of the words, all conduits joined in. Adie mouthed the words unconsciously.

The recipients began chanting in the same vein but different words. Adie looked over to the candles as the brightness in the room dimmed. There was no one near them.

Her stomach dropped when she saw Billie's fingers pinching the air, the lights diminishing on her simple gesture.

Billie had received the power of fire.

Billie had taken her place.

Adie tensed her stomach, weighing down her body as she stayed seated in the pews with the children and the unallocated residents.

Being chosen to receive the magic from the conduits was also a gift, and a curse. Once received, you could never truly be free of it.

Conduit or recipient.

Although the tablets helped. At least that was what they were designed for.

But everyone wanted to be a receiver of the magic, either as a conduit or a chosen recipient. When Adie had stopped being part of the true town, she saw what it really took to be one of Mr Kenjins' chosen ones. Bowing down to whatever the Town Leader wanted was primary directive number one. The more you were a 'yes' person, the more hits of magic you received.

Fumbling with the small bottle, Adie didn't count the number of pills that fell into her hand before throwing them into her open mouth. She gagged as a tablet hit her tonsils, but swallowed them all dry in the end. With the bottle tucked back into her pocket, Adie shoved her hands beneath her thighs and closed her eyes.

The chanting grew louder. She knew the incantation of transfer but kept her teeth and lips clenched tight.

It rumbled around the walls. The ground beneath her feet shook vibrations up her legs. She trembled beneath her skin; the chanting loosening her organs from the one thing holding her together.

The real fear came from inside.

She wanted to rub away the suffocating warmth in her chest, but she would not let her hands out. They itched to soothe the discomfort within. She fought them, keeping them trapped. Not strong enough to keep them entirely still.

Fear flooded her.

This feeling. This *fear.* As raw and dark as all those years ago.

The tablets. Why weren't the tablets working?

59

She had once commanded the powers she felt vibrating around the room. She hadn't wanted them. But she hadn't wanted to live without them, either.

And she now yearned daily for that power. It created that hole inside of her, that never stopped waving and demanding attention, suffocated her into this half-life.

The scars under her sweat bands itched, and she remembered how helpless life was without the connection to the town, the connection to the power, to the magic.

But she shouldn't be able to feel the vibrations in the room. The tablets stopped all her powers. Didn't they?

Sweat beaded on her forehead and she looked around, eyes desperate to find someone, anyone who could save her. She needed to stop the electricity burning beneath her skin, flowing to her fingertips, heat burning beneath her thighs.

Memories from that darkest of nights slammed against her. She felt the cold steel pressing against the warm skin of her wrists.

A wave engulfed her, smashing her soul against the rough grains of wet sand. Adie gasped for breath as the chanting reached its crescendo and stopped.

Always so sudden and all at once, a connection between all in the room. One mind, one thought, one goal.

The power had been dispensed, the eyes of the recipients would shine, and the exhaustion from the conduits would be palatable.

The silence pressed on her ears, throbbing.

Her body shook, her hair prickled over her arms and neck.

Adie dropped her head, the shaking slowly ebbing. Eyes closed, the sobs wracked through her chest as the magic in the room found its place and the ritual was completed. The feeling of that power drained away from her with each exhale.

Adie had seen the ritual enough times. But she had never felt this. She had never shared her magic, except for that one time, in private.

It was a horror she had nothing to compare it to.

It was a horror she would never live again.

Even the memory of it sent her body into a panic. The way Mr Kenjins had scoffed, had not believed her about receiving the power. He chose the conduits of the town. She had clicked her fingers, and he saw the flames. His eyes had looked almost black in the shadow of her fire. He had held her down, his hands rough and careless, chanting the words. The magic had been pulled and ripped out of her.

Two hours later she had pressed the razors into her flesh. She had cringed but didn't stop until the blood flowed. She had laughed, high pitched and unnatural, as she watched her secret waterfall no one else would ever know about.

But they had found her.

They had healed her, even after she screamed at them to stop, even after she had set Dr Simms' hair on fire.

Dr Simms had forced the tablets down her throat and had kept her on suicide watch ever since.

Adie's powers had been gone before the next town meeting, her connection to the town and the people forever impaired.

The voices as they returned to normal conversations around Adie meant nothing. She was lost in the past, terrified about the future. If the powers were coming back, what would stop him from knowing, from taking it from her again and again? From having it ripped from her body to be given to others?

What would stop her from using the razors again?

When she came back to the present, Adie felt a macabre chuckle bubbling up her chest.

Her body may have stopped shaking but tears continued to fall into her lap, even as gasps of humourless laughter escaped her lips.

Her chest ached. Invisible fingers had reached in and squeezed all her organs until they bruised beneath calloused skin.

Adie's insides trembled; her skin prickled with goosebumps.

The magic was back: she could feel it burning and wavering inside of her. Flames of a campfire.

"Come on, Ads, let's get out of here." Billie's hand was its own fire against Adie's shoulder blade. She nodded without looking and let Billie weave her through the mingling crowd, out of the building.

The grass was a soothing balm on Adie's palms. The sobs came again, and she gripped the green blades, digging her fingers deeper into the soil. With trembling hands, Adie tried to undo her shoes. Billie gently pushed Adie away and slipped off Adie's sneakers for her. Adie took a deep breath and dug her toes into the ground while her fingers gripped again at the blades of grass.

"I thought I could feel it again. It feels like it's closer than it has ever been. I think I'm going crazy, Billie."

"Shhhhh, hush now." Billie rubbed her hand in slow circles over Adie's back.

Adie continued to dig her fingers into the grass.

The cut fingers on her left hand touched dirt, and the world shifted. Catching her breath, Adie opened her eyes.

The nightmare, veins of *her* nightmare, played in front of her, overlaying the real world. The differences were subtle, but Adie knew the nightmare intimately. She saw the withering flowers, the forests that no longer lay over the land. And the people, the glints in their eyes and the glow of their skin. She knew the glow, the familiarity she had seen just that morning.

Her breath came fast, her chest rising and falling too quickly.

"Adie?" Billie's voice was an echo down a long corridor.

Adie surged to her feet and ran, her soles not registering the cuts and scrapes.

She headed toward James Road.

Towards Tala.

Chapter 5:

The chain fell apart in a blaze of sparks under Adie's grip. The heat coursing through her veins and her fingers were a hot fizz, crackling with each movement, hardening her skin with a shrinking pain as though flames burned from them. The power raged inside of her, stronger than it ever had when she was sixteen years old.

Horror touched the back of her mind, but the power raced through her. The magic, the drug, finally relieving the anger and anxiety from years of abstinence.

"Who are you?" Her hand was around Tala's throat, her pulse pounding rhythmically against the webbing between Adie's thumb and pointer finger. "What. Are. You?"

"I—," Tala couldn't get enough air for words. Adie threw her to the ground, then stared at her own hands, mesmerised.

She had never hurt anyone else before, only herself.

It felt good.

It terrified her.

"I'm like you, Adie."

"Fuck you. You have his eyes, the beast from my nightmare's eyes. Tell me what's going on!" Tala smirked at Adie's words. Adie wanted to hurt her again.

"My eyes only look like his, because you are seeing it through your magic, seeing the same magic that's in you."

"What is going on?" Adie asked again. "The whole truth this time."

"You know what's going on. Deep down, you've always known."

"Known what?"

"Where does the magic come from?"

Adie felt winded. It was one thing to assume Tala's knowledge of the town's magic, it was certainly another to have her confirm it with such a confident and matter-of-fact manner.

Tala knew about the town's magic. Knew more about Adie than she knew about herself, it felt.

"It comes from the earth. The Town Leader is given it by our goddess, and he distributes it to those who are deserving, those who would love Mother Earth and maintain her, those who have pleased the goddess." The words were empty. Hollow.

"And you believe that shit?" Tala laughed, hard and angry.

"I don't know, okay? I don't think anyone really knows where it comes from."

65

"Oh, *someone* knows. The magic isn't given. It is stolen."

Adie offered Tala her hand. Their eyes locked and for a moment Adie's body swayed a little in time to the flickering flame in Tala's stare. When Tala's fingers touched Adie's skin, the swaying stopped, the spell broken. The heat of Tala's body felt close enough to ignite the sparks in Adie's stomach, and lower, until Tala blinked.

"Tell me everything." Adie's voice came out soft, yet raspy.

"I can't. I can only show you why I'm here. And only a little bit. I don't have Diana's strength." Adie flinched as Tala drew even closer, hand raised, reaching up to Adie's face. "I can show you, but you have to trust me."

Adie swallowed hard. She had to be brave, she had to risk this. The answers were worth it.

She hoped.

But *trust.* Trust wasn't so easily granted.

The image of Lisa that had been on the edge of her thoughts since she saw the blood, moved to front and centre.

They were in bed, laughing as Lisa drew sparks in the air. Adie loved to watch the magic, to feel it wrap around her. Everyone else shunned Adie from seeing the magic. If they knew she watched them at the park, the scandal it would cause! But Lisa always showed her. She would dance it on her skin and smile at the look on Adie's face.

She hadn't been in love with Lisa, but she loved her, a caring friend and a comfort in a world where eyes drilled into her or worse, passed through her as if she didn't exist.

66

Lisa had given her what no one else ever would; safety. Adie owed her. She loved the pleasures and freedom that being with Lisa had given her, in a town of supervision and scrutiny.

"Okay." Adie had to hold onto this, believe it was all worth it, all worth *something*.

Tala didn't smile. Her angular face drew close enough for Adie to feel the warmth breath on her face as she pressed her palm against Adie's cheek.

***

"Are you really going back?" Tala sat cross-legged on the end of the hotel room bed, facing its twin where Diana zipped up her small bag. The grey and orange comforter appeared mismatched with the broken side table that sat between their pillows.

"There's something there, Tala. As soon as I stepped into the town, I could feel it." Diana's voice was deep, and perfect for radio.

Her beauty lingered after her voice faded. Diana's dance lessons were evident in her every movement, though her limbs were long and angular, flowing like a river.

Tala and Diana were chalk and cheese. But their eyes were identical. The only thing that recognised the two of them as sisters.

Tala had never dreaded any of Diana's missions, but the foreboding of this one would not be shaken off. There was something in OpenFields, she could feel it even three towns over. This was what they did: they tracked down the old ones, the forgotten ones. But this mission felt different. A heavy pendulous cloud hung over her, hung over Diana and OpenFields. Diana had simply laughed it off when Tala had first mentioned it, but the cloud had stayed put.

Diana left, and three days passed. Three days of pacing. Her neck felt raw from rubbing her hand back and forth over it.

Three days and she had smelt the metallic tang of murder in OpenFields.

They hadn't been on official business for The Children. Diana chose to investigate this without Tala. Now she was missing, and Tala had to act.

She would have to go in alone.

She couldn't ask for backup; it would take too long to explain everything to her people, and that was assuming she would be given help even after that.

Diana wouldn't go radio silent without a very good reason, and Tala hoped it was all the silence meant, a choice on Diana's behalf as she scoped out the town, nothing more than that.

***

Adie gasped as Tala pulled her hand away from her face. She fell back into her own body, the sharp glare of the sun making her wince after the dull evening in the hotel room, while her body felt too crowded.

How did I do that? Tala's thoughts resting behind her eyes for another moment, before drifting away like vapour.

"She's your sister." The only information from Tala's memory that didn't raise a thousand more questions.

"Yes, my baby sister." Tala's voice was quieter than Adie had heard, but the gruff rumble was still present.

Adie was pleased with the revelation.

Not now.

"Who are The Children? Children of what?"

"You shouldn't have heard the name," Tala stared at Adie, eyes wide, the deep depths filled with a fear Adie didn't think possible.

"Why not?"

"They were my thoughts. I only showed you what happened. It's just... dammit, forget the name," Tala snapped. "We need to find Diana and Lisa. And then I'm taking her far away from this town. Someone else can deal with the mess."

Tala shivered; Dedo Rock felt as cold as the town they looked down on.

"So, I'm just supposed to be expected to be okay with this? You have magic, you know our town has magic. How?" Adie asked.

"Do you honestly believe your town is special? That magic exists here and nowhere else?"

Adie opened her mouth to answer and quickly snapped it shut again.

She had questioned where the magic came from, but she never asked if it was floating anywhere else in this world.

"Look." The touch on her arm made Adie flinch. Tala's hand moved back just as quickly. "Things are never

69

as simple as you think they are. But you don't want to get involved in it."

"I am involved in it." Adie's voice was quiet, and for a moment she wasn't certain if she had spoken the words aloud. "I want to know where the magic comes from. Where is it stolen from? I've always wanted to know the goddess. I didn't understand why only the Town Leader got an audience with her; it didn't sound right. But no one would listen to me."

"You..." Tala stepped back, shaking her head. "You really don't know? I thought that was just a town act. Is that why you are shunned?"

"What? No, they hate me because I had the magic, but I couldn't deal with it." Adie plucked at her wrist bands. "They lost my connection when I was no longer a conduit. Looks like I've finally been replaced now though."

Tala sat down on the ground with a heavy expulsion of air.

"What do you mean?"

"You mean there is something you don't know?" Adie felt the left side of her lip lift in a half grin. A flirty half-grin.

This is not the time for flirting.

"How does OpenFields work?" Tala asked, her piercing eyes focused.

Adie sat down on Dedo Rock, looking over the patchwork of a town she loved and hated, despised and cherished, and told Tala the world she was raised in.

"We are all able to receive the magic, but only some of us are gifted enough to become conduits. Mr Kenjins visits

70

with the goddess and depending on how pleased she is with us, she gives him the essence of magic. I don't remember when Mr Kenjins gave me the essence from the goddess, but I have so many moments of blackness in my life it doesn't really matter. Those who receive the essence become conduits. We... no, *they*, transfer the power to the others."

As she spoke, she knew she shouldn't be telling an outsider, yet felt freer than she ever had in her life.

"What moments of blackness?"

"I don't remember anything from before."

"Before what?"

"I wasn't born here. They found me when I was six." Adie had never had to say it before. Everyone in OpenFields knew her story.

"And it's all blank?"

"Yes."

"Convenient. Are there other moments?" Tala asked.

"Some, but just little ones. Nothing important."

"How do you know that? How long has Mr Kenjins been running the town?"

Adie was surprised at the sudden change in the conversation, but the relief was also palatable on her tongue.

"Since before I got here. It's been passed down through his family since the town was established. His great something or other was one of the original miners."

Tala closed her eyes and Adie stared at her, taking the opportunity to really examine her features. Her eyes were tilted up, slightly angled, lashes from eyelids to eternity. Adie was drawn to the cupid's bow mouth and had a moment of imagining biting the full bottom lip.

Stop it!

"We have to find Diana and Lisa now. And I have to report back to The Children as soon as we find the source of the magic."

"Children of what?" Tala's response was a glare. "Fine, but where do we start?"

"At the source," Tala replied, glare vanishing. "Close your eyes and then open them slowly, focusing on nothing but the magic."

"I told you, I don't have the magic anymore."

"Yeah, you do."

"What?" Adie knew Tala's words rang true; she just didn't want to admit it to herself. Her magic had returned, stronger than before.

"I can smell the lavender in the pills you have in your pocket. It's covering up the ingredients that are dampening your connection. But they aren't working anymore, are they? They were infused with your Doc's magic. When she died, so did their power."

Tala was right. They weren't working. Was she right about the pills being magically infused? It made sense. And what did she have to lose by trying what Tala asked her for?

"Okay, I'll do as you ask."

Adie took a deep breath and closed her eyes.

Slowly, she opened them as instructed. It was like a flashlight piercing the midnight darkness of her mind. Adie yelped and closed her eyes again.

72

Tala's hands were a comfort on her forearm.

"Slower. You can do this."

Adie counted to ten and tried again, slower, one eye at a time, fluttering before opening them.

Beginning at the field behind her house, Adie trailed the dark smudge, pushing her magic at it to burn away the black insidious ink. She followed it to the centre of town. As she stared, the mass thinned out and, lit up like a beacon, was the town hall. Fire and ice burned inside her chest as her breath laboured, tears choking in her throat. She wanted to laugh and cry. It was home and prison cell in one.

It wasn't a surprise, and Adie had to resist the urge to smack herself in the forehead.

Where else would it be?

Mr Kenjins had always been possessive of the town hall, as though it belonged solely to him.

"Please, tell me what is going on?" Adie forced her eyes away from the glow. Tears slipped over her cheeks and ran in rivulets that tickled. Her hands trembled as she brushed gently at them.

Tala started pacing. Three steps forward, three steps back. Her lower lip pushed to one side of her face, her teeth forcing her lip to stay there.

"Okay." She stopped pacing and squatted down in front of Adie, excitement in her eyes making her look crazy or stoned, maybe both. "What if all those old religions were right?"

"What?" Adie scoffed and shook her head.

"Hear me out. Remember. You wanted this."

73

Adie felt warmth swell in her lower stomach but nodded.

"Okay, so let's say there are Gods, and Goddesses, but what the religions got wrong was the nature of the gods. They aren't divine, just a different race. Far more in tune with magic, in tune with the world and able to wield certain elements by sheer will, through their very blood."

Tala waited for the information to sink in. Adie nodded.

"Go on."

"Now, what if humans found out that their gods weren't immortal or infallible?"

Adie knew the feeling too well, betrayal and anger. Pressure in her chest pushed her memories from that night to the forefront of her mind. Mr Kenjins was nothing more than a fraud, hungry and greedy for power, enough to steal it from a child. She had been in the pews with all the rest, looking up at him, this father figure...this *god* of their religion.

Tala nodded but said nothing.

"They would feel angry and like fools. And," Adie tried to rush through the patterns she knew about the human race, rush through the things she had wished in those moments of pure hate for that man, "they would want to get their revenge. And what better way to do that than to steal the power of those they once bowed down to, grovelled to, prayed and confessed their sins to?" Adie knew this with more certainty than she had authority to. It was a clenched fist in her stomach.

74

"And others would fall in love with these beautiful creatures." Tala replied, staring into the mid-distance.

"The Children." Adie gasped.

Tala only nodded as she sat back down next to Adie. Adie processed this information as though it were fact. She believed it, despite how crazy it sounded.

Is it really that crazy in a world where OpenFields exists?

"So, what is the source?" Adie heard her blood raging in her ears.

"We have to go." Tala jumped up quickly and pulled Adie to her feet.

Her eyebrows knit together. She had more questions. But then the sound of tyres on the dirt road made her understand.

Someone drew near.

She ignored the electricity as it ran through her fingers. Adie gripped Tala's hand tighter and pulled her toward the other end of the overlook. Was the electricity attraction or magic? She couldn't remember, the magic had touched her for so short a time. That and the lingering effects of the tablets still dampened the edges of her thinking.

"Where are we going?" Tala asked, voice tight and urgent.

Adie hustled her further down a walking track that was almost entirely reclaimed by the surrounding bush.

"We are taking the scenic route back to town. This track circumnavigates around to my place. A short walk to town from there. And with the sun setting, no one will look for me."

"I guess that depends on how far the cops have gotten."

Adie nodded. She shouldn't have forgotten about them.

But she wasn't worried. She hadn't been raised to fear them, not when they were in her town. And despite what Mr Kenjins said, no one would help them find the truth behind OpenFields.

She could feel the pulse of the earth through her bare feet. Her body vibrated with fear and excitement.

Her fingers reached into her pocket, gently stroking the plastic bottle of pills. What was the point when they had stopped working, anyway? And yet, there was still comfort from the plastic smoothness.

"That's my place." Adie jerked her head toward the small abode as she walked past it and toward the open grass field where she had seen the misty figure this morning.

Was it just this morning?

Her world had turned upside down in less than twenty-four hours.

"We should go in and rest up, wait until later when everything is truly dark and still before we head to the town hall," Tala whispered.

Adie wanted nothing more than to go in, have a shower and a cuppa tea. Instead, she shook her head.

"No, we can't wait there."

Tala followed silently, a question on her full lips.

They sat down on the grass behind Adie's house as they watched the last few fingers of the sun disappear over the horizon. Adie shivered, wondering if they sat in the spot where she had seen her waving figure.

What a horrid omen it was turning out to be.

"Why didn't we stop at your place? Shoes would probably be a good thing." Tala spoke as darkness settled around them.

"When I became a conduit, when I first felt the magic, I wasn't happy about it, but I did the right thing and told the Town Leader." She spat the title. "He tried to force a transfer of power on me. I don't know if that's what he does to everyone. But he lied. He claimed he chose who received the power. He would never have chosen me, the mongrel of the town. But I could feel it pushing against me, begging me to hurt him, I could see myself using the magic to kill him. And so I stopped and let him take whatever he wanted. Everything after that felt wrong and strange. And dark. Above everything else, it was so dark. I got a blade and tried to take the darkness away."

Adie pulled off her wrist bands and showed Tala the scars beneath. Tala gasped and Adie lifted her eyes.

Their eyes met.

Tala's gaze slipped down to Adie's wrist. Her own hands tentatively moving forward. Adie nodded, meeting her halfway.

Tala's fingers gently ran over Adie's skin. A lump formed in Adie's throat. Tears building, ready to run over her cheeks.

"Since they took the magic, they put me in that house, and have monitored me every day of my life. They got me to work in the library with Lisa."

"Why didn't you just leave?"

The tears came faster, and too many things that she had never even allowed herself to think came rushing to her mind.

"I wish I knew." Adie's laugh was filled with pain. "I've thought about it, I've even tried. But I want the magic back. I hated it, every second of it felt wrong. But if I left, I would never get it back again. That would be it, all gone forever. Nice and crazy, huh?"

Tala's hands finally dropped away from Adie's wrists as she laughed.

Adie roughly brushed away the tears with clenched fists before pulling her wrist bands back on.

Adie hadn't shown anyone her scars, not since the wounds healed. And now this woman was laughing at her. But the anger and the disgrace of her actions surrounded her.

"I'm not laughing at you. I think what you just described is so beautifully real and human. I'm a little envious." Tala murmured with a gentle smile.

"Of me? I am nothing to be envious of."

"You are. I wish we had met in some other circumstances."

"If we had met in other circumstances, I wouldn't have been brave enough to talk to the sexy and confident woman who controlled every room she walked into."

Tala laughed again and raised Adie's hand, kissing her fingers.

"I'm sorry." Adie had a desire to bury herself in the ground. It was the magic all over again, feelings so right and so wrong overwhelming her. Lisa, she cared about Lisa, she loved her. But here was Tala, a stranger who knew her better than Lisa ever had, even after all those years and nights of whispered pillow talk.

"Please don't be."

"What magic do you have?" Adie needed to know. This wasn't her. Since she met Tala, she felt both more and less like herself than ever before.

"What do you mean?" Tala's head cocked to the side as she asked the question.

"I can't lie to you. I've just shown you what even Lisa hasn't seen. I am saying stuff I never say." Adie quickly closed her mouth, knowing if she left it open, she would simply continue to spew whatever words came to her mind.

Tala laughed, a rich deep sound that lit her face and her eyes. Adie couldn't help but smile. Laughing suited Tala.

"My powers are only in making you see what I want you to see. And I'm not sure I really have that much power over you. You knew I wasn't a cop before the real ones showed up." Tala smiled, met Adie's eyes for the briefest of moments before looking back to the horizon.

"Besides, you aren't the only one not keeping as quiet as you should be. So, do you have anything useful in that backpack or have we been dragging it around for the fun of it?" Tala asked.

79

"You mean, you didn't snoop when I was in town?"

Tala smiled and shook her head.

"Just the usual stuff. My staff access card, a torch, a bottle of water, wallet, muesli bar. Random things I have forgotten to take out of it. That kind of thing."

"So at least some of it is handy."

"It's getting dark, we should head off now. We've got to find Lisa and Diana." Adie forced the words over the lump in her throat.

She had never felt this connected before. Not to Billie or to Lisa.

There was something different between her and Tala. Too many thoughts brushing against her mind. Too much information, too much confusion.

Puzzle pieces were being dropped in front of her, but none of them connected with each other.

Tala helped Adie to her feet.

Adie closed her eyes, unable to watch the trace of lines Tala made as she lingered at Adie's wrist bands. The magic was back, and so was the darkness.

Chapter 6:

Darkness smothered the town hall. Billie's home, Mr Kenjins' house, backed on to the town hall so the chances of being seen, of *getting caught*, were likely, but the lack of daylight would help conceal them.

The tension ran up and down Adie's body, electricity and fire beneath her skin.

What Adie couldn't quite believe was how much she loved the sensation. Excitement replaced fear.

She silently chastised herself. Why had she stopped asking, stopped searching for the truth, for the source of their magic? Adie should have known the town hall stood at the centre of it all.

In her mind, she could almost see a wall, built between her thoughts and knowledge that hadn't been able to be breached for years, too many years. But the wall had crumbled. Brick sized holes were starting to appear.

Her fingers trembled as they touched the bottle in her jeans.

She knew why she had stopped asking.

"Break into places often?" Adie's voice was muffled as it pressed up against Tala's ear. Her skin radiated with nerves as Tala picked the lock on the front door of the town hall.

Adie's hand shook slightly, the light from the torch bouncing around on the front door.

"I have many skills," Tala smiled. "Now hold that thing steady."

Adie grinned, attraction mixing with adrenalin.

Sound bounced around the empty streets as the lock gave in to Tala's insistence.

They froze, waiting for a call to halt, or a scream. But the echoing clicks died down, and after another thirty-second count, nothing else happened.

Tala turned the handle and waved her hand for Adie to go first. She slipped into the internal darkness, the soft carpet a warm relief to her feet.

"Where to?" Tala asked, scanning their surroundings.

Adie took a deep breath. She knew.

She grabbed Tala's hand and led the way. Down the hall towards Mr Kenjins' office. The mysterious always-locked door, even when he lurked inside.

She remembered one day when Billie had hurt her leg, a scar still raised just below her knee. Angry, she had watched Billie be chastised instead of comforted when her father reefed open the door after five minutes of knocking.

82

That had been the beginning of the end.

If that was what having a family was, Adie was grateful to not remember her own.

It was a subtle shuffle, different to the lightness of their own tread. Adie and Tala locked eyes, questions and answers passing without words. Again, the soft sound. Adie's breathing sped, her chest rising and falling. Tala's fingers were warm, almost as warm as Adie's own as they squeezed them with a slight nod of Tala's head.

Adie whipped around and pinned Billie in the glare of her torch light, Billie's own torch making Adie blink. She crossed her arms, holding them up in front of her eyes, still making sure her light illuminated Mr Kenjins' daughter.

"What are you doing here?" Billie's voice hissed.

"Right now, I'm trying not to be blinded."

"Adie?" Billie's voice shook a little as she lowered her torch.

"Who did you think it was?"

"Another detective." Adie could just see the thrust of Billie's chin toward Tala as Billie spat out the words.

"No, me. I'm with Tala. What now, Billie? You going to go report me to your dad again?"

"I was only trying to help you." It was years ago, but still Adie held the anger like a ball of fire in her chest. She was done, she was free. But Billie was the one who knew something was wrong, the one who called her daddy and with Dr Simms' help, brought Adie back to this nightmare of magic and pills.

"Yeah, well, I don't need your help. Just piss off. We'll be out of here soon enough."

"You just broke into the town hall." Billie had the upper hand, and she knew it.

"So, go and tell daddy." Adie didn't have time for Billie or trying to play nice. Their time limit of getting in and out just decreased incredibly.

"So, you haven't heard? Why would you, alone on the outskirts of town..." Billie blushed in the torchlight. "He's not my dad."

"What?" Adie's head swam. Was nothing she knew real? Bile rose in the back of her throat. How that man held knowledge to his chest as though it belonged to him and no one else. Did this explain his disdain toward his daughter, or would he have been just as detached from Billie if she carried his blood? Adie's world had changed forever since the morning.

"Mum had an affair with a visitor during the Carnival of Flowers. It's why he's never trusted me."

"I'm sorry." Did it mean they had a few more minutes after all? Adie thought down a blush at the thought. She could see Billie's hurt. "What are you doing here?"

"I found this." Billie handed something over to Tala instead of Adie.

"Where'd you find this?" Tala's voice was rumbling, barely holding on. But to what, Adie wasn't sure.

"My dad had it, I figured he forgot about it."

"What is it?" Adie couldn't make out the item passing between the two other women.

"It's Diana's." Tala handed the heavy silver lump to Adie, pressing it into her hand with too much force. "It's her blood."

"How do you know that?" Billie looked closer at Tala.

"She knows it. She's not a cop, Billie. She has magic as well. And she came here to look for Diana." Tala glared at Adie, who could only shrug. "It's either this or she runs and sets off an alarm."

"I'm not telling anyone you are here." Billie's voice dropped to barely audible. "I know where Diana is."

"She's alive?" Tala's voice cracked and rose.

"Last time I saw her, yes."

"Do we trust her?" Tala asked the question Adie didn't know the answer to.

Billie's eyes blinked in minimal light and Adie remembered a time when she would have done anything for her.

Now she wasn't even sure about vouching for her.

"What choice do we have?" But Adie knew she had a choice. She could turn around; she could forget it all. She could leave this place.

But none of that seemed like a real option.

"Come on then, before he gets back." Billie bit the words out.

"Gets back?" Tala asked.

"Town Leaders meeting in my house," Billie smiled in a shy way. "It's why I knew it would be safe to come here."

Billie turned and Adie followed her. After a few steps, Tala's grip on Adie's arm stopped her in her tracks.

"Shh."

Adie nodded in response. Billie was still walking.

"She smells of Diana, she could have been the one to hurt her."

"Billie's a coward," Adie replied, frowning after her old friend as she disappeared into the darkness of the town hall.

"And often they are the most dangerous."

Chapter 7:

Does everyone know how to pick locks except for me?" Adie's words spilled out in a nervous rush as they caught up with Billie, on her knees picking the lock of her father's office.

"Probably." Billie's half smile sent an old feeling of familiarity flitting through Adie's body. But it was followed by sadness.

Adie looked at the woman in front of her and felt nothing but the *memory* of fondness. Her friend had idolised the cruel man parading as her father. Everything she did was in the hopes of pleasing him, making him proud. She couldn't imagine what Billie was feeling now. To discover the reason for his disdain was something she would never be able to overcome. What would that do to a person? It explained so much, and the guilt gnawed in the pit of Adie's stomach. She should have forgiven her. After all, she had just wanted to save Adie.

Billy achieved the criminal act as the lock popped, and Adie almost laughed. It was so anticlimactic. The heavy, smooth wooden door swung open and revealed the most generic of offices that Adie could ever have imagined. There was nothing spectacular about it. She wasn't sure what she had expected, but nothing so... *normal* had entertained her imaginings when she was still a curious child of the church, and she fantasised about what lay behind Mr Kenjins' door.

Perhaps a big glowing neon sign saying 'yep, I'm the bad guy' or something similar, perhaps even a candlelit altar with bowls of overflowing blood would have appeased her.

Instead, she discovered a square box with a desk, chair and filing cabinet all facing the door they entered. Along the left-hand side of where they stood sat a two-seater couch.

Tala's grip was once again on Adie's arm. She didn't need to look at her; she knew exactly what she would see.

The room looked normal, but she could feel it. Adie noticed the raised hairs on Billie's arms.

It would seem none of them were immune to the metallic, tainted magic that stuck to their tongues.

"Where is it coming from?" Adie asked.

"The couch." Tala seemed confident.

Billie nodded and stepped up onto the cushions; one foot on each seat.

"I haven't been in there for years, I don't know what we will find," Billie whispered.

"Just open it," Tala commanded.

Adie looked sharply at the woman. Her words had come out like thunder in the distance. Then Billie pressed the palms of both hands against the wall.

For a moment, nothing happened. Adie expected, perhaps wanted, someone to jump out, hopefully Diana, and tell them they had all been pranked and the whole town was in on it.

Instead, the wall gave in to Billie's pressure. It moved back just enough to reveal a weak light around the edges.

"What the fuck is this? I feel like we've stepped into another dimension." Adie felt the hysteria in her words, trying to bubble out into laughter.

"We've always been in this dimension, Adie. Dr Simms just softened the blow for you." Billie's voice was hard and seething.

"You know about the tablets?" Billie played a part in Adie being put on the magic-dousing pills, but she didn't realise her old friend knew about them. More secrets and lies.

"Yes."

"And you never told me?"

Billie's teeth clenched, and she glared at Adie for a moment.

"Dr Simms didn't want you killing yourself. My dad didn't care either way, but you became her little obsession."

There was nothing Adie could say. She had been used. Why and for what purpose, she had no idea. Was she just a guinea pig for the tablets? That familiar burn sparked in her chest. She should be used to the betrayal. Had she really expected anything else? But still, she rubbed her chest. How much more could she handle before the flames used her own bones for more kindling?

Mr Kenjins controlled who became conduits and who received the power. Why had the tablets even existed? The tablets that weren't the secret she was assured they were.

But if the power had been stolen... stolen from what and who? The goddess. The goddess she had prayed to. Screamed at so many times. Did she even exist? Tala seemed convinced.

Answers that only led to more questions.

Adie began to question everything, like she once had. What was Mr Kenjins getting out of sharing the essence with the conduits? It didn't make sense. And she had followed them, she had stopped asking. She was just another sheep. The only choice she had made on her own had been taken away from her, the night that saved her.

"Tell me what happened to Diana?" Tala's voice sent chills up Adie's spine; it held the deep rumble of a war cry.

Adie was impressed Tala didn't have Billie by the throat.

"I heard Dad and Dr Simms fighting the night Dr Simms was killed. She was screaming at him for being so careless and thinking of himself a god. She mentioned the reporter and told him the interview was his stupidest move yet."

"Is she alive?" Tala grated, face like granite.

"I don't know. Diana came for dinner. She left." Billie shrugged. "I didn't think anything more of it until I heard Dad and Dr Simms fighting."

"Where did you find her necklace, Billie?" Adie forced the words out evenly. It wasn't adding up. Adie wanted it to, oh how much she wanted it to.

"It was under his desk when I was cleaning up."

"In there?" Tala's voice sent tendrils of fear down Adie's back.

"I clean once a week, when he's in there working."

"He didn't see you find it?"

"No."

Adie and Tala looked at each other. Neither of them spoke, but Adie saw the reflection of her own doubts in Tala's eyes.

"How did you know about the pills?"

"I hear things, I live in the house where all the meetings happen. You think they'd learn to keep their voices down occasionally."

"Enough, let's get this over with." Adie's voice was a lot stronger and in control than she felt. Listening to Billie bitch about her lot in life was too much to swallow.

Neither Billie nor Tala argued with her, yet she almost hoped they would. She had never been a fighter, but she was itching to hit something, *anything*, right now.

The three of them stepped over the couch and pushed the concealed doorway open. From within they were confronted with a deep blackness that cut through more than sight. It burrowed into Adie's mind and thoughts. It was

91

metallic to taste, and the anger in the air was a pressure against her skin.

The darkness settled over them as they stepped into the hidden tunnel. Adie was glad neither of her companions could see her face.

Her fear had turned hysterical inside her mind. Memories from every nightmare, waking and asleep, danced on the edges of her sanity.

If she had a mirror, she was certain it would be a look reminiscent of The Joker or other such insane characters.

The Cheshire cat on speed, perhaps. She stopped and willed her face back into neutral submission.

Tala took the torch from her hand and led the way inside the dark unknown.

Adie let out a slow breath and blinked as white mist wafted out from between her lips.

"It's so cold."

"It's Diana." Tala placed a warm hand against Adie's cheek. Her body reacted before her will could stop it, closing her eyes and leaning into the touch. "She has mastery over the temperature. It's one of the reasons I knew she was still here. Come on."

Tala nodded, pulled her hand away slowly with her fingertips lingering a moment before removing themselves, and led the way into the dark unknown.

Chapter 8:

Adie had taken little notice of what Tala wore. She had simply glanced to find her in a suit, fantasised about removing it. But as she followed, catching glimpses of Tala ahead, she focused more on the specific details. Tala wore a long jacket with deep pockets. Every time Tala turned back to check on those behind her, Adie saw the black pants and pale blue button-down shirt with a collar that looked almost white in the gloom of the tunnel.

Tala's magic obviously had a bigger effect on Adie than either of them realised.

With practiced ease, Tala swept the torch beam back and forth, hitting the tunnel walls and picking out the path in front of them.

Adie didn't trust Billie behind her, but it was better than having the distance from Tala. She had never felt so like herself as when she was with Tala, the Adie she desired to be; so confident and strong.

49 steps in, Adie wondered if she would ever stop counting her steps. Tala stopped, holding up a clenched fist in the half-lit darkness. Tala walked around an enormous obstacle and looked over the top of it to Adie.

Adie didn't like the look on Tala's face.

She moved to stand beside her.

In the torch light Adie saw the obstacle become the yellowing whiteness of bones. Billie joined them. Adie stood shoulder to shoulder between the two, and as Billie added her torch to the light, Adie saw clearly what they were all looking at.

A pyramid of skulls stared with empty eye sockets at them. The pile was deliberate in every placement, and all skulls were devoid of their outer remnants. No flesh or skin remained, no hair or tell-tale marks. If there were any cracks or defining features, the shadows concealed them.

"They aren't real. They can't be real." Billie's voice trembled as she turned off her torch.

Adie knew Billie was hiding something, but the fear of those skulls appeared genuine. Adie's own fear was buried under a flash fire of red-hot anger. Deaths. More god-damned deaths. Were these all murders as well? Had murder been in OpenFields all this time, beneath the surface?

"They're real. And so are those bodies." Tala stepped away with the light, walking further into the tunnel and leaving Adie and Billie beside the pyramid of skulls.

Billie collapsed on to Adie's chest, sobbing as her torch dropped to the ground and rolled away. Adie wrapped her arms around her, making shushing noises, not knowing what else to do.

"What's going on in our town, Adie? What's that man really been doing?" Adie tensed slightly as something false in Billie's words hit her ears.

"He's your father."

"No, he's not."

"He raised you. How do you really not know what's been going on?"

"She does know." Tala's voice was a rolling thunder from the darkness.

"Good girl, Billie. You might prove to be my child after all." The nasal voice of Mr Kenjins hit Adie's ears moments before his snarling face came into view.

One fist was tangled up in Tala's hair, while the other twisted Tala's arm behind her back.

Above them, a small glowing ball of light bobbed and lit up the tunnel.

Adie turned to Billie and was met with Billie's fist, crunching into her face.

Chapter 9:

The pain in Adie's nose made her eyes water as much as the crunch that echoed inside her head made her feel sick.

The smell of fresh blood filled the air.

"Better actress than I ever gave you credit for." Adie spat blood on to the floor, her stomach curdling at the taste.

Her legs gave way, and she fell on her knees, hard dirt and rock gashing the skin. She had fallen beside the bodies Tala had spoken of. White limbs stuck out of rags that might once have been clothing. If the remains were any sign, the bodies had simply been dumped, no rhyme or reason, just excess flesh and bone with nowhere else to dispose of them. A shudder forced its way up Adie's back as her mind, playing tricks, superimposed her own body over the bones. An image of her younger self, blood drained from slashed wrists. Would she have ended up here, just another skull for a pyramid that made every sense and none whatsoever?

"Get her up." Adie didn't resist as Billie followed her father's command and pulled her to her feet, dragging her after Mr Kenjins and Tala.

"I'm sorry, Adie. But I don't want to lose the magic."

"Fuck you, Billie!"

"You'll understand soon enough."

Adie bit her tongue on repeating her witty response. She understood all too well how it felt to lose the magic. It was the waking nightmare of her life. All she wanted was to get her and Tala out. The small hope she had for Lisa was dying.

"So, you helped kill Dr Simms? Why?"

"I didn't lie to you, Adie. Not a word of it. I found the necklace when I was cleaning, and I heard dad yelling at Dr Simms."

Adie's hands curled into fists, her short nails digging more crescent moons into the skin of her palm. She had no choice but to keep up with Billie, the woman's fingers bruising her arm. Billie needn't have worried, if anything, Adie wanted to up their pace. They were falling behind and losing sight of Mr Kenjins as he continued to manhandle Tala. Their footfalls still echoed back to them, a relief in Adie's chest as she listened to the constant heavy clomp from him and a more subtle press onto the earth from Tala. Her and Billie's own footsteps kicked up debris, and the hollow echo of rock and dirt surrounded them.

"But then what? You showed your dad? You helped him stage Dr Simms' murder in her office?"

Adie felt vindicated as she saw the flinch and cringe in Billie's face. Was there still hope?

"It was an accident. And I haven't been down here since I was twelve years old. The skulls weren't there."

"The skulls and bodies are human beings, Billie! Killed by your daddy dearest. You still think Dr Simms was an accident?" Adie shook her head. Her neck muscles tensed. She turned her head away from having to look at Billie any longer.

They walked on in silence.

The tunnel ahead sloped downward, and as they followed further beneath the ground, the air grew colder until too soon, Adie could see her breath white and cloudy in front of her.

A different energy lurked beneath OpenFields. It wasn't the beautiful honouring magic that they were all baptised in.

It was dark, angry, and frozen.

What if hell really wasn't the burning pits everyone liked to think? What if hell was a frozen wasteland, and it was coming up to claim OpenFields for its own?

The thought came to Adie, not from her own thinking. She shook her head. So many questions and no answer, just more questions. Another intrusion into her thoughts as they drew closer to another patch of darkness shaped like a pyramid. Hair on Adie's arms stood to attention and she wanted to cry and vomit.

She squinted ahead, trying to force herself to look beyond another triangle of death. A smudge in the darkness floated before her and the skulls, as though an artist had rubbed the heel of their palm across a pencil drawing not yet set. Blinking away the film and with a small shake of her head, the smudged edges began to lighten. Slowly, as her eyes adjusted more to the intrusion of the gloom, the figure from her morning greeting floated into view. Recognisable but just as blurry, as though still too far away.

Adie's head whipped to Billie's face. Billie's eyes narrowed in confusion at Adie's look, perhaps even in question.

"Tala?"

"Yes. I know." The word vibrated from the darkness, filling Adie with a warm calm and knowledge.

Air washed over Adie's lips in a shudder of sharp shards, It was the pressure in the air that had been building up for weeks now. The cold snap that was too early for this time of year. The unseasonal weather that told Adie the exact time of Diana's death. The pit of her body rolled like the angry sea. Her anger, or Diana's? Perhaps both.

"Shut up." Mr Kenjins' voice was high pitched and sounded completely unaware of the weight of the simple exchange. Adie almost laughed out loud.

They came to another, a third pile of skulls. These were still white, they had yet to yellow or become stained from the dirt of the underground tunnel. The skulls and the triangle they had been arranged into sent a shudder of fear and loathing through Adie.

The magic inside of her reacted to them.

But the clothes and the bones were far worse.

The bile was rising a burning trail up her throat as she found some less deteriorated scraps and recognised the uniform, the same one she put on every weekday morning.

They had all been disgruntled teens, working just enough to earn their way out of the small town. She had never imagined that not one of them had ever actually escaped. The number of times she had envied them their freedom.

Her mind screamed to turn and run, but she couldn't, even if Billie's vice grip fingers weren't digging into the flesh on her upper arm. She couldn't turn away now, no more than she could every night when the nightmares settled upon her.

She placed a hand on the top skull in the triangle, said a silent sorry for those she no longer remembered the names of, and pushed with all the strength she could muster. It seemed like such a childish, useless act, but somehow vital.

A rumble called from the darkness in front of her as Mr Kenjins screamed and Billie pulled her away from the toppling skulls.

The rumble in Adie's chest was almost audible, as though a rock band had turned all their amps up to full base.

"Get her under control, Belinda."

Billie's grip increased on Adie's upper arm. Adie smiled in the darkness as she was forced further beneath the town, the tunnel continuing to decline.

The ghost waved ahead of them. Adie knew who it was now; her heart ached for Tala. Adie caught glimpses of

100

Diana's ethereal form every dozen or so steps and felt the first sparks of hope.

Another large dip into the earth and Adie's breath caught in her throat. The cave was dark and veined with colours she couldn't quite catch or name.

She had always been alone in the nightmares. The nightmares had seemed so real in every aspect except one. Not once in the nightmares did Adie's claustrophobia play a part. Not once did she truly ache for the sun and the cool open breeze. It was that knowledge when she woke that helped her remember. It was all just a dream.

But now, the walls now pressed around her. Her hands beaded with sweat, despite her breath still puffing out in white clouds in the freezing air, the veins of half colours only increasing the pressure on her chest.

This was not the same. Now, she walked into it. The place of her dreams.

The nightmare had never been just her imagination. She had always known it: she had always pretended that she didn't. She had pretended she believed them when they said it wasn't precognitive. It was easy to imagine beasts and fantastical things in a town where magic truly existed. It had made sense, and she had believed the lie.

Adie may not have chosen the path that led her here, she may not even be here of her own free will, but that didn't mean she couldn't make a difference.

She needed to know, and she needed to stop whatever was happening in this town.

The deaths of all those people, nothing could justify that.

The triangle had meant something, something Adie should know. There were still too many bricks in that wall in her mind.

Old knowledge that had been trying to make its way to her pushed against her thoughts. It was so close. She tried desperately to remember the books Lisa had shown her, to remember anything that hinted about these old gods, this race of powerful beings. But there was more than the books behind that wall.

The coffin, the stone coffin, the one in her dreams. It forced its way to the front of Adie's mind. She gasped and stumbled in her steps.

More bruises on her arms from Billie's iron-like grip as she pulled Adie onward. No time to think. The soles of her feet stung as she landed on jagged rocks and hard packed earth.

Adie's eyes adjusted more to the darkness, and the lights that throbbed through the darkened walls illuminated the path in front of them with a regular pulse.

Dark and light.

Dark and light.

Dark and light.

There was a heartbeat in the veins.

The latest pile of skulls and discarded bodies illuminated and then plunged back into darkness.

This last triangle was much smaller, not yet completed, but on the top of the half-formed triangle was a head with blonde hair that made Adie shiver.

She heard the sob float from in front of her and imagined the anger and pain in Tala's wail.

Despite Adie's desire to keep her eyes on the darkness, she turned to look at the face of the head that topped the triangle. Standing beside it was the ethereal body, head attached, a transparent version of the necklace she still held in her hand, resting on Diana's chest. The silver wolf's head glowed bright against the ethereal form.

"She didn't do us justice; she was an enemy to OpenFields." Mr Kenjins' nasal voice was closer to Adie. Tala had slipped from his grip and was now on her knees beside the tower of skulls, sobbing. Diana's ethereal hand was gently stroking Tala's shuddering back.

Mr Kenjins seemed unmoved by Tala's collapse. His gaze seeming to pass through the spectral image of Diana.

"I didn't think there was anything wrong with the article," Adie snarled.

"She called us a cult, like we were some kind of frauds."

"You aren't a fraud. You're a murderer," Adie spat.

"I'm faithful to this town. Their lives were meaningless until I granted them a purpose."

"You are so clichéd." Adie's skin trembled beneath her clothes. She was impressed that her words didn't show any signs of the quivering she felt inside. "You going to say we'd be nothing without you? And what of the goddess? Just a fiction of your own creation to justify your villainy?"

A look flashed across his face. Unreadable, but it twitched the corners of Adie's lips. "Take care of this one. I'll keep going with Adeline." His words were clipped and as unfeeling to Billie as they had been to Adie.

Billie barely nodded, letting her grip on Adie's arm drop and moved to stand over Tala's sobbing form. As Adie stepped past, running her hands over Tala's shoulders, she felt the strength of tensed muscles. The tears were real, but the anger beneath so much stronger.

"Lead the way, head toward the end." Mr Kenjins' words were too relaxed, too sure of himself.

"And why should I?"

"Because you want to know what's down there." The arrogance in his voice grated on Adie's nerves. It made it worse that he was right.

"I know what's down there."

"Good, let's see if you're correct. Get moving."

"No."

Mr Kenjins lifted his hand and Adie's feet left the ground in unison.

With a thud, she hit the wall of the cave. She landed on the floor opposite Billie, Tala, and the pile of skulls. Pain radiated through her right shoulder from the impact. It streaked up through her neck and slammed against her skull like a police raid on a druggie's front door. She sagged in the darkness, alone and powerless.

Chapter 10:

No one resident should have that much strength and power. That was the reason they were rotated weekly. That was the reason they were given for the change and switch of recipients.

Adie had never heard of the magic being used as a weapon. The magic was all based in nature; protective and life giving.

"You're a conduit."

Adie should have guessed, should have *known*.

"A conduit who never shared the power with the town."

"No, I'm a leader. I am granted what I need to keep this town perfect." He strutted over to where Adie half lay, half crouched against the wall.

"The private transfers," Adie scoffed and had she had the physical strength to do so, she would have slapped herself in the head. "Every one of them gets sent to you. I wasn't the only one."

Adie laughed, biting her cheeks to keep back the hysteria and the exhaustion wanting to overtake her.

"You aren't special, Adeline. Just a little orphan suitable for my purposes. You're lucky you ever got a taste of the magic. I simply took what was always mine."

"But you can't be a conduit, can you? The essence doesn't work for you."

"Not anymore. There is a finite amount any one person can consume." Mr Kenjins growled, scowling down at his shoes, heavy black boots splattered with mud and darker purposes.

"That makes it sound like you don't steal the magic."

"He was going to take the beast with him. He spoke about the entire world needing a touch of the magic. But here, we could make our town perfect, instead of spreading it too thin. I use it for the better of our town. Now get up and get moving."

He? What exactly was he talking about? Who was he talking about? Just play along.

She hadn't known, she had never known where the knowledge came from. That knowledge that itched at the back of her mind. That now glowed through the brick sized holes of the wall.

The coffin.

Adie got up, Mr Kenjins at her back, as a few more things fell into place. She hoped Tala really did have enough strength and wits left to deal with Billie.

"Okay, so I'm going to die, obviously. At least tell me what the hell this is all about."

I know more than you think, and I wanna see how much you're going to lie.

"Like I'm some kind of villain in those stupid movies?"

"Well yeah, kind of. But I'm still on the tablets. I don't have contact with the magic."

Please don't know about the tablets. Don't turn around, don't show him your terrible excuse for a poker face.

"I'm not the villain," Mr Kenjins said. "I'm the hero. I'm the reason this town didn't just disappear into oblivion when the gold ran out."

"The gold in the mines ran out long before you were born. Sorry to tell ya, but you had nothing to do with saving this town from oblivion."

She heard his scoff behind her. Adie always felt so stupid around him. She was always the last to know everything in OpenFields, it felt.

He jabbed her in the back, keeping strong, not giving up his heinous reasons or plans. Every now and then he would prod her again as her feet shuffled and she tried to slow the progress toward every nightmare, toward every hell.

They were moving further into the cavern. She knew she had to face the beast, face the darkness, all the nightmares that had led her there, but still she feared the walls and the cavern.

"You know what, I actually don't care." And the truth of the words surprised her as she spoke them, turning on her heel to face him, to let him see the truth in her eyes. "Whatever psycho reason you have for all this, I don't care.

You are nothing more than a murderer. And for what? To keep a town beautiful? You are seriously cracked."

Mr Kenjins smiled, a cruel one that didn't reach his eyes. "I am not cracked."

His hand barely moved, but the power he wielded whipped against Adie's cheek, splashing her blood onto the dirty ground. "Enough."

"Why not just kill me?" Adie didn't want to die but delaying walking into that cavern was all she could focus on.

"You're a conduit. Any conduit can replace the beast, to keep the magic flowing through our town. Your pills will run out and the magic will return. You will do your part to keep this town alive."

"You're lying. I can see it in your eyes."

"The beast will die. And you will take his place."

A sob escaped her mouth.

For the chains or for the beast's death? It made no sense she would care about the torment of her nightmares. But there she was, making promises to herself not to let the beast die.

"Why do you think I will help you?"

His smile flickered in the light and for a moment Adie saw teeth sharpened to points and fear dropped cold acid on her spine. Like the portrait of Dorian Gray, the darkness revealed the true nature behind Mr Kenjins' face.

"You don't remember where I found you. Oh, I was near the end of hope. After two-hundred years, the magic was thinning out. It was barely keeping this town alive. But then I found his kryptonite. The beast has never retaken his

108

human form, even then, but his ward against his mind lifted and I saw you. All these years, asleep in the forest."

What is he talking about? Two-hundred years?

He pushed her backward, toward her nightmare. She turned just in time to put her hands down in front of her. Adie caught herself from falling directly onto her face, stopped herself from crashing into the rough ground. Sharp rocks stung her palms, but the pain was irrelevant.

She was in a recess in the ground. An imperfect circle that, as she followed its curve with her eyes, led toward the end of the tunnel, the other side of the bulging cavern, where a dark mass rumbled noises that vibrated up through her hands.

The scene washed over her like a tidal wave.

Everything was similar to what she had seen night after night in her nightmares, but not quite the same.

Was something missing? Were there more things she never noticed in the nightmares?

The beast snarled louder, and Adie closed her eyes, swallowing over a raw lump in her throat.

She wanted to run.

She wanted to look up into its face and know why it scared her so much.

Her eyes opened, but her gaze froze on stained hoofs. They were rubbed raw and bare of fur, sending up clouds of dust and dirt as they stamped into the ground.

Adie let out a slow, icy breath between pursed lips as she lifted her head slowly. She'd face the nightmare like a woman.

109

Chapter 11

The beast loomed, pacing back and forth in the alcove of the cave, the roof above him slightly lower than the rest of the open cavern. His hoofs shuffled at the lip on the other side of the indented circle. Adie froze, still on all fours, staring at her incomplete nightmare.

His movements were limited to the thick chain that attached back hoofs to the wall. And even though she had seen him thousands of times, with his wild eyes and canine grin, the sight of him sent a fear that tried to liquefy her bowels.

She took in every detail of him, details she could never focus on in the nightmare.

His matted, dirty fur gave hints of a lighter bronze colour. She imagined it would have shined beautifully in the bright light of day had it been washed and brushed and taken care of. Giant clumps were stuck together, matted with a black ooze that Adie could almost smell.

It was a stench to make her gag. A mixture of faeces and blood.

The biggest shock came when Adie continued to lift her head, and her eyes met those of the beast. The fire in those eyes was dulled by the film of milky cataracts. Adie stared, unable to pull her eyes away from his gaze, and the eyes cleared, just a little, just enough to truly see her.

And for her to see him.

The kindness and the pain radiated toward her, and she ached inside for the beast who had once traumatised her nights.

From the corner of her eye, something moved, something that was never in the nightmares.

"Lisa?"

Lisa's hands were handcuffed in front of her. She was kneeling on the rim of the recessed floor, a cut above her brow dripping blood over her swollen left eye.

"I'm sorry, Adie."

Adie looked between Lisa and Mr Kenjins.

"Sorry for what?" She didn't want to hear that the one person in town she trusted was also in on the murders, on the control.

"Mum and I were looking into something. Something to do with you. I should have told you."

"Yes, but that's not really the issue right now." Adie's words were softer and gentler than she had expected. "Are you okay?"

Lisa let out a small laugh that held no humour, but she nodded.

Mr Kenjins chortled and shook his head. "How very sweet. As if you actually care for each other."

Adie's face didn't hide her surprise fast enough. And in true Mr Kenjins fashion, he misread it, believing he knew all there was to know.

"I know everything in this town, Adeline. That's what makes me the veritable god. And I control everything. Do you really think it was Lisa's idea to have you work in the library? She's been my little mouse from the first day you started working there."

Just like a villain in one of those stupid movies. Kenjins couldn't let any of his master's movements be seen as someone else's choice. 'He.' Adie. Remember the 'he' Mr Kenjins mentioned. Knock him off balance, he'll reveal all, he can't help himself.

"So, you told her to fuck me?" She raised her left eyebrow, hoping it looked nearly as impressive as Tala made it so effortlessly look.

She silently begged that Tala had taken care of Billie. Adie wouldn't mourn long over Billie's death. She was certain Billie wasn't involved in the actual murders, but did that matter? She hadn't done enough to deserve any less.

"I told her to do whatever was needed to be done for the greater cause, for this town." But his eyes flicked with a dark glare toward Lisa.

"So that would be a no." Adie laughed, a small sharp noise that felt like a stranger's.

Adie felt alive and electric, the warmth inside of her comforting amid the cold air surrounding them. With it

112

came a sense of hope, that sense of being far more than just their pawns. And there was a rumble inside her chest.

But she was too tired, too sick of feeling used and abused.

She looked to Lisa, unsure if it was a wink or Lisa trying to flick drops of blood from her eye. Adie wasn't sure it mattered either way. People had died. Human beings had been murdered.

Lives that mattered.

Despite the weight in her limbs. Despite how she felt. It wasn't over until her heart stopped. There were too many questions still left unanswered. She needed to know, she needed to be sure.

The building pressure of the town's storm was pushing against her head, against every memory and thought she could remember. It relieved Adie to hear that she wasn't special. That she was just there. But she couldn't just let it happen. She couldn't let it keep happening.

"Who is the man?" Adie's voice quivered like a small child's. Everything ached. Her cut feet and hands, the throbbing of her shoulder and neck. But the rumble in her chest was insistent.

She was so tired.

But she couldn't stop yet.

She had to find him.

That had been what was missing. That was the rumble in her chest. It was him. Calling to her.

There was no man here, she couldn't hear or feel him. In her memory she saw his angled eyes and face, his anger and exhaustion. He was present in every nightmare.

But there was nothing in the cavern. No man, and no coffin.

"What man?" Mr Kenjins hissed as he stepped closer to the beast, then stopped more than two metres away. Adie looked down at his boots, at the earth that cradled them.

Had Lisa felt him? Did Lisa know? Was it a wink after all?

The beast stopped pacing and collapsed onto the ground in a thud against dry packed rock. Adie saw its ribs through drooping skin covered in scars. A fresh wound lay across his back legs and her heart wept for his pain. He wasn't well, he wasn't the true beast of her nightmares.

The nightmares were not her own, they were the man's and the beast's. They had been calling out all these years, screaming for help. And she had never listened.

"What man?"

Kenjins' shrill scream didn't force her to answer.

Adie got to her feet, everything aching. She wasn't sure he needed the answer more than he needed her alive. But if he wanted to kill her, it was going to be on her terms.

She pushed the thought aside and focused on each step.

Adie walked toward the beast, hand out as though to pat him. Mr Kenjins screamed for her to stop. She didn't. Not until her hand rested on the beast's marked hide.

The images swept over her in a rush.

Mr Kenjins stood in front of the beast. Behind them, a scene of beauty filled the world. There was an underground waterfall, shining with a light that bloomed beneath the froth. The waterfall roared with a clean perfection, filling Adie's ears and breath with a calmness she had never felt before in her life. Yet it felt so familiar. So safe.

The walls were veined with rainbows of colours feeding into the water. The beast was healthy and strong, with eyes kind and gentle, with just a little, just a touch, of fear and anger.

In Mr Kenjins' hand a whip with spikes flashed toward the beast and cut lines into his hide. The beast roared and tried to run toward Mr Kenjins. Chains pulled him back toward the waterfall where he fell, blood dripping into the water.

"You will give me the magic." His voice was still nasal but with a youth Adie found hard to reconcile. "You will help me make my world perfect again."

The beast snorted a hot puff of air from his nostrils. It took a moment for Adie to realise Mr Kenjins was being laughed at.

The beast paid for his insolence.

The blood dripped from the beast's body. Mr Kenjins caught it in small vials he tucked into his jacket.

Adie watched in horror as time sped by. The waterfall's glow receded, and then the water itself. The pit of earth grew smaller until it was the mere recess she was in now.

And all the time, the visits from Mr Kenjins, whip always in hand, sometimes thrashing at the beast without *asking a single question. The vials were all filled and still he continued to flick his wrist; the smile widening across his face, his eyes gleaming with his pleasure.*

Time continued to speed by, people on their knees, heads bent over the indent before Mr Kenjins' knife slit their throats. And then sawed through the bones, taking the skulls back into the tunnels with him.

There were still questions as Adie returned to the present day. Mr Kenjins continued to scream at her, but he had yet to take a step closer.

How long have you been here?

Adie asked the question in her mind, hoping the beast understood.

Each new step was a gamble. But it was this way or Mr Kenjins'.

Adie was happy to bet on the unknown. Her hands shook and her heart raced. Still, it was better than the devil standing behind her.

He is older than he looks. He has lived more than three lifetimes when he should have only lived one.

The words were a relief and a horror. Adie's eyes stung as they widened.

Lifetimes he had been chained and beaten, deprived of the sun and the feeling of the cool breeze brushing past and through his fur.

I'm so sorry, Adie projected. *What do I do?*

I cannot tell you. I don't have control over humans' actions.

116

Are you a god? she asked, her mind spinning at their connection.

Adie's hand brushed over the beast's fur. Were the muscles beneath rippling with enjoyment or fear? The fur was gritty and hard under her faintly stinging fingers; the cuts closed but not quite healed.

How were they healing already?

"Get back from him. You will not touch the beast any longer." Mr Kenjins commanded; his voice touched with panic.

"If you want to stop me, come and get me." Adie called his bluff. Mr Kenjins' face paled.

Yes, child, I am a god.

An old god? Adie asked, ignoring Mr Kenjins.

My name was lost and burnt away. But you once called me Pha. I am just one of many who keep the land, the animals, and the waters in harmony.

"Tell me of the man!" Mr Kenjins' scream was so loud Adie wondered if dogs were now reacting somewhere above the earth.

"Oh, shut up!" she yelled, sick of the pathetic little man and his games.

Adie turned back to Mr Kenjins as fear and excitement crashed inside her chest, waves beating against the rocks. There was too much power, raw and vibrating under her skin. Sparks, like a fire trying to be lit with flint and stone, leaped from the tips of her fingers. Memory of its warm caress flooded through her veins. The fear came later... Adie watched the sparks and heard Mr Kenjins' intake of breath.

117

She smiled, the pull wide enough to sting the edges of her lips.

She raised her hand and flicked it in Mr Kenjins' direction.

She watched the man, awestruck, as he flew through the air and hit the wall of the cavern with an audible *whhhooopphh*. Her hand trembled as she looked at it and felt the urge to pick up the unconscious man and throw him again and again against the rocks until blood poured from him. Fear reigned in the adrenaline as she looked up and met Lisa's gaze. She looked at her with slack jaws and wide eyes. But she knew Lisa didn't fear her, even as Adie feared herself once more.

She wanted to see Mr Kenjins' brains and matter, everything that made up this cruel and vile human, shattered and broken. He deserved it. He deserved worse.

But she didn't deserve the guilt or the nightmares.

She balled her hand into a fist and focused on the beast's body as it shook beneath her.

"I won't hurt you." But as she spoke, she knew her error. He was not shaking out of fear, but with laughter.

She could hear a second laugh, a man's weak chuckle.

"Did the magic turn Kenjins into this?" She spoke the words, her head pounding at the temples. Would the magic turn her?

No, the magic is neither good nor bad. His nature always held this possibility. The possibility is in all of humanity.

118

"He doesn't see the man. I thought you two were the same, but you aren't, are you?"

She sensed the head shake and while she wanted to ask more, she could feel his breathing become more laboured beneath her hand. Her fingers trembled and tears built in her eyes.

I am not done yet. I have something for you.

For me?

A memory. Adie swallowed over the lump in her throat.

There was no cave. Adie was lying down, looking up, catching snatches of the blue sky, playing peek-a-boo between the gaps of leaves in the forest canopy.

"Why must I go to sleep, Pha?"

"Because there is danger, and I must find Marcell and get us all safe. But sleep until I return."

Adie closed her eyes and felt the warmth of the sun leave her skin. Her breath caught and tears slipped through her closed eyelids. She opened them a crack and saw the cement covering her. Hands reached up and touched the cement. Small hands, that of a child. A slight sob escaped her young lips as she opened them to call Pha, when darkness pulled away from the memory.

The images faded, and Adie returned to herself.

I was entombed? She didn't want to ask, but she needed to.

Yes. For as long as I could keep you. For your safety.
Will you release me?

She nodded, glad to think of something other than the coffin. Squaring her shoulders, Adie stood taller against her

119

fear. She didn't want to live like this, drained of all her power, *trapped*. The word was a lump in her throat, in a world where her claustrophobia could never be removed, but could she live with herself, leaving him there?

She didn't think so.

Is it true? Any conduit can release you?

No. She sensed the chuckle.

But I can?

Yes.

Will I still have any powers once you are released?

The powers are yours. They are yours to do with what you will.

Even after all of this?

Adie shook her head as she spread her arms wide to encompass the death of the landscape around her and the shuffling Mr Kenjins who was now coming to his senses, not quite standing up, but pulling himself into a sitting position, resting his back against the pulsing wall.

Even after all of this.

"What do I do?" she asked, speaking out loud.

She had decided she would not go back on her word. Perhaps she would get used to the cold that continued to make her tremble.

You step toward the wall. You must see beyond it.

Her feet fought against the movement.

She was willingly stepping into the nightmare, taking his place, claiming the nightmare as her own.

She would sacrifice her existence. Adie would suffer to give him relief, she would suffer as a price for his freedom, as retribution for all he had endured.

It wasn't something she ever thought possible of herself.

A life she would never experience flashed across her thoughts.

Friends and family, a Christmas tree she could lie beneath and fall asleep under, a dog snoring on her feet, dinners in restaurants where no one knew her name.

All these possibilities were gone in an instant.

All these possibilities were never any closer at hand.

She stepped again. The air tingled against her skin and the world warped around her.

The beast lurked behind her, and in front of her she saw the man hanging limp against the wall. And around him were statues and the coffin.

Her coffin.

Chapter 12

She had forgotten the statues.

She took them in, one by one, pressed around the edges of the cavern, layers thick. Some were crumbling, falling around newer ones.

How had she ever blocked them from her memory? It was an unwanted skill she had for some time if the vision of her entombment was true. And she knew it was.

Their glowing red hearts throbbed behind the black statue stone. Even those that were crumbling continued to have the same ruby red pulse within them.

"Are they the hearts of the dead? The bones out there?"

"Yes." Pha's voice was gravel scraped back with metal. It was the voice in her mind. He was a frail, limp excuse of a living man. Was he a man? Hair like ragged seaweed, dirt and stubble that bled together, no definitive mark of where one stopped and the other began. He was the personification of every pirate movie she watched as a kid;

the starved and half-drowned rat who had been chained in the prison of the ship the entire time. But his eyes were alive and strong. A darkness that held promise and threat in one glance.

She shivered. They had been speaking through the beast, but now they faced one another.

"Why?"

"To drain our powers," Pha coughed out the words. "He learned that once the waters were drained, he needed human blood and the power of the triangle to keep us here, and to keep us alive. I brought the souls in here with me so he could not find a way to abuse them as well."

"And my...my coffin as well?"

"Not a coffin child, a stasis chamber. I did not imagine you would be trapped in there all these years. But I felt it when he touched the blood against the lid. He woke you, and time had stolen your memories. But I took the chamber before he could return for it."

She had heard enough, seen enough. She had seen too much. Her fill of horrors had well and truly overflowed.

Although she knew they were nowhere near finished yet.

"Can he see us?" Adie asked. He gave the smallest of head shakes to the negative. "Why can I?"

"You have the blood of the gods. My blood."

"You are my father."

Pha nodded and smiled. She could see it, even behind the stretched skin and dirt. Features she only saw in the mirror. She had imagined finding someone else reflected back once she escaped this town. If she ever escaped this town. But to find them here, under her feet, literally, the entire time? And for so long a time. Two-hundred years asleep, abused. Tortured by Mr Kenjins. It was too big.

She focused instead on the man in front of her. Tears burned her eyes as she blinked them back. This hardly seemed the meeting of her childhood fantasies of family and belonging, but still there he was. Her father!

With a shaky breath, Adie forced her eyes away and looked at the statues once more.

"Are any of them still there? Can we bring them back?"

"They are there, but trapped, not able to be returned to their old lives." He shook his head as he spoke, such heavy weighted sadness in the movement, in the deep rumble of his voice.

"What do you need?" Adie wasn't sad; she was well past that. She felt a wild fury, and for once she no longer cared how angry she was, or how close the darkness inside of her was to coming out. The fire that burned felt right for the first time.

Her hands remained still, her heartbeat steady and even.

"Water." The word was barely audible, his head lolling forward as though the minimal conversation had drained what little energy he had.

"Oh, of course." And as simple as that, the darkness receded just enough for her humanity to remember the pain and imprisonment this god had suffered. Her *father* had suffered.

His bones were so close to his paper-thin skin. She could see each rib and every breath. She found the water bottle in her backpack and pulled it out. Unscrewing the top, she held the metal cylinder up to his mouth.

Pha gulped it down and the hearts surrounding him throbbed brighter.

"Where did she go?" They both turned their attention toward the raging nasal fury of Mr Kenjins as he beat clenched fists into the body of the beast.

"I can stop him." Adie wasn't certain she could, but she felt the power surging beneath her skin, and she suspected she was stronger than she knew.

The fire had returned in full force, and she was looking to burn some revenge.

"No." Pha's voice still sounded like a rusting robot, but there was a hint of strength now. "Marcell is no longer in pain, I have removed him from that body."

"I'm so sorry."

"He is my guardian, my conduit, and my familiar. Above all, he is my friend." The god's voice was thick and slow, no hint of the fire that was burning hotter and hotter inside of Adie's chest.

Adie shuddered.

He couldn't be ready to give up the fight. Her sacrifice could not be in vain.

Adie would not leave him here while he still had breath in his lungs. Time pressed against her.

"How do I release you?"

"You already have. All I needed was one of the triangles to be destroyed, and water in my veins again." His arms fell limp beside his body and Adie ran to help him as he pushed against the wall to help him stand up.

She noticed the marks identical to the whip lashed scars on Marcell.

"How do I get you out before I take your place?"

"Oh, my child." He chuckled, a container of pebbles being shaken by children's hands, and pressed a rough hand against her cheek. "You came through thinking you would replace me?"

She nodded, unable to speak over the lump in her throat.

"No, this town needs to end. I might have been caged, but I still have my claws. I can send you away, you do not have to see any more horrors."

"No!" Weight sloughed from her shoulders. She had given up on the fantasies of a future, of a life outside of tonight, outside of the cave, outside of OpenFields. A spark lit inside her chest. She would stop the nightmares of this town, and she would find a way to stop the arsehole himself, somehow.

She would not turn away, tail between her legs.

She would see this end; she would know first-hand what happened to the town she loved and hated in equal measures. Her life was not as important as that. But she would fight and hope for life. If she lived, she would hunt down the answers to the questions that continued to scream in her head.

126

"Ah," he called out as his legs buckled beneath him. Adie grabbed the man, the god, her father, to stop him collapsing completely to the ground.

As he leaned on Adie, pulling himself back on to his feet, he gasped again. She felt him inside her mind. All the horrors her life had been since she felt the magic, since she became a conduit. The fear that wrapped around her when Mr Kenjins held her down and syphoned the magic from her body. The private transfer he said was normal, he said was part of the goddess's wishes.

"I'm sorry, child. So very sorry. My gifts were never meant to torture you." Pha's voice cracked with fresh pain.

"I never understood what was happening. I never understood the nightmares you sent me, what you were trying to tell me. But I'm here."

They shared smiles and Adie gasped as the god glowed, a shimmering golden air around him.

"You have an aura around you as well, you are glowing with your strength." His head cocked. Was that curiosity or fear in his eyes? Shaking his head and closing his eyes, he smiled before opening them again. All traces of what was there were now gone. "You are important on your own. Everyone has the potential to be. It's our actions that make us special, not our blood or our lineage."

"He has Lisa." Adie tucked the information away. She would deal with that later... if there was a later. They weren't finished here yet.

They both turned and faced the world outside their thin veil of protection.

"Then come. It is time for this to end."

He grabbed her hand, and she felt the fury and the fire burning within him. She felt relief and an angry pleasure as his fire helped to build her own higher with greater heat and intensity.

"Concentrate on the veil."

She saw the glimmer of the veil waver in front of Mr Kenjins as he kicked Lisa to the dusty ground.

"Where's the man? Where did that little bitch orphan go?" Mr Kenjins' voice was beyond high pitched—shrill—as he asked again, lifting Lisa back to her knees with one hand as he grabbed her by the hair, pulling her up with his fist. Lisa's smile was bloody.

The veil cracked open in a rain of frozen shards. The cold blasted away from them, their heat raging and roaring through the cavern. Adie and her father stepped toward the shimmering air between their reality and the ravaged world.

She controlled the fire once more. She felt the darkness, dove into it and gasped for breath.

Her father's hand gripped her fingers tightly.

Mr Kenjins turned and stared in confusion at the scene in front of him.

Ice shards were quickly melting as they surrounded a man he didn't remember ever seeing, holding hands with the very orphan bitch he was screaming for.

Chapter 13

The confusion didn't last long, nor did it make him release Lisa's hair.

He turned, pulling her with him. Her head was now pulled back, her eyes staring at the ceiling. Lisa's shirt was ripped open with lines of beaded blood soaking what little of the material remained. In his other hand he raised that spiked whip, ready for another strike against Lisa's torn flesh. Adie hadn't seen it hidden behind his body.

Adie could see better in the dark than she did previously. She could see glistening beads of aorta blood dripping from the black leather and landing with small thunks on to the thirsty earth. It soaked up her blood as Lisa laughed.

Adie recognised the hysteria.

She pulled her eyes from Lisa to the beast, Marcell, and then back to the man. The man who was her father. Pha.

She gasped as his chest bled from a whip's lash and realised what it meant.

"You're linked with Lisa?"

"Yes."

"How? Why?"

"Lisa is hiding in her mind. Marcell's body was about to give out. I transferred him to share with Lisa. We are linked mentally, but the bodies we inhabit are influenced by that. Hurt one, the other hurts, too." The gravelled voice sounded smoother, water and purpose having softened further the friction between stone and metal.

"Move away from her." Mr Kenjins' voice rose as it echoed with force across the swollen cavern.

"He has used up the last of the magic he has taken into himself. He never learned moderation," Pha mumbled. Adie picked up traces of a dark laugh beneath.

Mr Kenjins laughed in turn and lowered his arm. Lisa cringed, but her eyes locked on to Mr Kenjins before shifting to meet Adie's. Lisa was still there, but behind her eyes was something darker and older.

Adie smiled, touched her fingers to her lips and blew her fiery breath on them.

Mr Kenjins screamed. Lisa sobbed, her eyes following Mr Kenjins' arm as it tore and flew away from his body, the whip handle still clenched in his fingers. The blood was warm and hissed against the coldness that surrounded them. The arm and whip landed by Adie's feet. She stepped on the wrist until the inert fingers released their grip.

Adie watched, without flinching, her hand now pressed against the fading warmth of the beast beside her, tears running over her cheeks for the pain she could feel radiating from him, even in death.

Pha let go of Adie's hand and stepped with the pure purpose of revenge toward Mr Kenjins as he sobbed and screamed abuse and empty threats.

Adie watched, pleasure tickling at her darkness, as Mr Kenjins was pulled apart, screaming and begging for the same mercy he never gave to Marcell over the centuries of torture, the very mercy he never gave to any of them. Adie watched as the other arm joined his first on the ground at her feet.

Tears streamed down Mr Kenjins' face, wet and thick, and guttural screams escaped his mouth, begging for forgiveness.

The god ignored the pleas.

Mr Kenjins' legs snapped beneath him, bones breaking and piercing through flesh, before being ripped from his body with invisible forces he couldn't fight against.

His screams echoed and bounced around them.

The god grew in size and light as his anger and revenge rebelled against his years of captivity. Behind him, the statues crashed to the ground, throbbing orbs of red rushing at high speed out of the cavern. Some raced down the tunnel, while others buried themselves directly into the ground above them, creating light shafts and breezes of fresh air.

The darkness was fading. Adie no longer needed to tap into her powers to see the reality of the surrounding decay.

It was heartbreaking and anger-inducing knowing, having those memories inside of her, when life was lush and beautiful outside.

"Adie."

The word, her name, brought Adie back from the darkness.

She was mesmerised by seeing and feeling the pain and the anger Mr Kenjins was suffering.

"Adie, help me."

Adie let out a happy sob as she saw Tala trying to lift Lisa's unconscious body from the ground.

"Help me with her, she's barely breathing." Something new burned behind Tala's eyes.

Perhaps it was always there.

"Give her to me." Adie lifted Lisa into her arms, smiling at how easy it was to take her weight. She had never explored the gift of her blood. She had no idea of her true power or potential.

Tala wrapped Lisa's arms around Adie's neck, making sure she was securely attached.

"We must leave now." Pha said. Mr Kenjins' sobs continued to echo around the cave.

Pha's skin was golden, his bones no longer visible, but he was still thin and frail to look at.

"Stay close, Tala." Adie moved to follow her father, but he turned, eyes sad and frightening.

"She cannot join us."

"Fuck you!" Would Adie be punished for swearing at her god? Would her father punish her? What punishment was there for the children of the gods? "She comes with me."

Adie drew closer to Tala, shoulders brushing against each other.

"Not *me*, Adie. He knows me; he wouldn't leave me here." Tala spoke quietly, but that didn't lessen the impact of the words.

"He knows you?"

"I'm a child of the gods. He can feel my blood, just as I can feel his, and yours. We all have eyes that bear witness to the history of our people."

"You knew this whole time? You knew I was one of The Children?"

"Not completely," Tala grimaced. "I wasn't sure it was you, or stolen blood and those stupid pills."

Then the meaning of Tala's words sank in. "I'm not leaving Lisa," Adie snarled.

"She's gone." Pha's voice was sad, but there was no arguing with it. "Marcell is keeping us both alive. The final act and power of a familiar. He is sharing his life essence with me. But it will take all our strength to get us out of here, we can't bring her as well. We simply aren't strong enough."

"Why can't we help? My power is strong, so strong. I can feel it. Use it, use Tala's. Please."

"I can't."

"Lisa." Adie sobbed and held the small frame tightly to her chest.

"She fought against him. She revealed nothing, though she could see me. She received a lot of my blood offerings. She died well."

If Adie thought she would be punished for swearing at a god, her thoughts of slamming a fist into his face would undoubtedly be frowned upon.

"Diana will guide her." Tala's hand was gentle and warm on Adie's skin. The touch made the tears flow, but Adie laid Lisa gently down on the ground. She hadn't noticed that Lisa's chest had stopped moving in and out.

While it hurt, relief also washed over Adie. The decision had been made.

Her life had been filled with fear of the darkness inside of her, but now she saw the lightness, and more importantly, she *felt* it.

Inside there was still a breakable heart that remained soft and warm.

"I *did* love her."

"I know." Tala helped Adie back to her feet and together, fingers entwined, they turned toward Pha.

"We must go." His voice was still rough and raw, but his authority was absolute. Adie couldn't help the sadistic smile that spread across her face as she saw the moment Mr Kenjins registered he would be left, limbless, slowly bleeding to death. A death that would linger and drag out as the stolen magic in his blood slowly oozed out and returned to the earth.

His screaming doubled, a blood curdling horror that despite him deserving his fate, sent shivers creeping up

134

Adie's back. The pleasure she had taken at seeing her father's revenge enacted now made her feel sick.

"Close your eyes," Pha commanded.

Adie closed them and held tighter to Tala's hand. Behind her eyes she saw Lisa's limp body, cut and bruised and damaged at the hand of their Town Leader. She saw the waterfall he had murdered and the piles of skulls, each representing a life that was stolen and used even in death.

She wondered if she would ever close her eyes and not see these things.

"Will it hurt?" Her voice was a whisper of breath.

"Did it?" Tala's hand was gentle on her cheek and she opened her eyes.

Carefully, Adie opened her eyes and turned to look over at the town as it rumbled in the darkness, shapes darkening against the dawning sky.

They stood, the three of them, near the edge of Dedo Rock, alone in the greying darkness. They could all feel the beginning of the new day. And they could all smell

Chapter 14

A soft breeze picked up. Adie shivered in delight at the feel of it brushing against her skin. Gingerly she sat down, the aches and pains of the day catching up and being felt through the adrenaline of the night.

Swinging her legs over the ledge of the rock, she breathed in the fresh air.

The man, the god, her father, remained standing, his eyes and concentration focused on the Town Hall.

Adie watched, her fingers spreading out as they pressed against her thighs, only for her to pull them back to a fist and repeat the sensation again. The sensation felt good beneath her shorts.

It was something tangible. Something that reminded her she still lived.

Eventually, the rumbling grew in intensity and the Town Hall cracked like thunder before it collapsed in on itself. A house of cards toppled.

Tala sat down beside Adie, their shoulders brushing against each other. She took Adie's other hand in both of her own.

The touch made Adie's eyes water, but she gulped the fresh air, forcing back the tears.

Adie imagined hearing the screams of the people in the town, but the wind wasn't blowing in the right direction. As far as she could tell, there was no longer any wind to speak of.

Many of them would now be woken from the earth's tremors. By the time they realised the true danger, it would be too late. For some, they would simply never wake.

They would be the lucky ones.

The town, building by building, collapsed in on itself, crushing the barren waterfall beneath them.

They had stolen its life and beauty for the town. It only seemed right that it would end with it all being returned.

Adie didn't know how many of them knew the truth of the magic. She should care. The innocent ones were dying for the sins of the rest. But she was too broken to spare a thought right now. Perhaps she would care in the morning, or next week, next month, next year.

The noises finally stopped as the sun finished its rise over the horizon.

"It needs to burn, Adie."

Adie nodded, wondering at the implications in the god's voice.

"Adie?"

Their eyes met, and she felt her mouth drop open. She shook her head, but his eyes pierced through her.

She had the power. He had given it to her. Given back what had been stolen. In her mind, the last few bricks of the wall collapsed, and the world opened up to her once more.

She was one of the children of the gods.

Taking a deep breath, she focused on where the library had been and sent her energy there. It was pulled from her, not unlike the night her magic had been siphoned by Mr Kenjins, but without the horror and the theft. She gave the magic willingly with a soft tearing inside of her. A heavy weight pulled at her arms and her heart. There would be nothing left to remember Lisa. No books with her handwritten chicken scratch in the margins, no colourful decorations she made in her spare time in that house with the stained carpet. It was necessary, but it didn't make the feeling any lighter.

She knew the flame existed. It was catching debris, but it was a while longer before the smoke and the fire were visible.

The magic felt right and pure, for the first time in her life.

Her shoulders dropped, her energy spent, and a small hiss escaped her lips.

Tala's hands moved over Adie's skin, and soon the pains and aches eased.

"Is that better?" Tala murmured.

"Yes, thank you."

"You have questions?" Pha's voice was soft, gentle.

138

Adie had almost forgotten he stood behind them.

Her father.

The idea was beyond surreal, but that, like regret for the innocent lives lost, was a problem for another day.

Her heart sank as she saw the truth.

She would not be able to save him.

"Marcell has held on long enough."

"I'm so sorry. All these years, I could have helped you. It was for nothing."

"It was everything. It is my time."

"But you are dying." Adie didn't bother holding back the sobs. She wasn't sure she would be able to, even if she tried.

It had all been in vain.

Dr Simms was dead. So too were Lisa and Diana. The bones of hundreds of others who had been killed for Mr Kenjins' power-hungry greed.

What had they actually achieved?

"I am, as must all things when their day arrives. But I am dying free, thanks to you."

"How can you die? You are a god."

"It is merely a word, an old word. We are but a race. A race that is dying. We once populated this world in greater numbers than humans. But we didn't know how to fear, or how to be cautious until it was too late. Now, I know fear, and I do fear that there are now less of us then there have ever been. And with men hungry for power, more of us die, more of us are used for what is our nature."

"More of your people are trapped?"

"*Our* people, daughter." He nodded, his eyes dimming as he sat down, taking deep breaths as he lay on the grass, a smile on his face.

"Daughter." The word tasted foreign on her tongue. "But who is my mother?"

Sadness deepened Pha's eyes and made them glisten, reflecting the flames that licked at the town below them.

"When we came to this town, we were fearless and helpful. When the Town Leader stole Marcell and trapped me, I put you in the stasis chamber, and a spell on him to forget. He had already drained so much of my blood by then, and my strength was not at its greatest. He forgot me, but he did not forget Marcell. You forgot as well, you forgot everything in the length of years between going to sleep and rising; an orphan, or so everyone thought. I'm afraid soon you will be. Your mother was the first victim of his cruelty. He killed her slowly and took her blood. But her blood was the strongest I had ever known. Despite his desire to hide the goddess from every one of those humans, she spoke of her love and her strength, her desires, whenever he let down his guard. She called to me and on occasion I rested behind his eyes, and I saw our child becoming more like her, and tortured by the same beast."

"I'm so sorry. I thought we had gotten to you in time."

"Do not be sorry. Without you, I would still be a captive. Now we can rest." His finger vibrated warm against her cheek, wiping gently at the fallen tears.

"How do we find them?"

140

"The sisters know," he shook his head, remembering, sadness creasing his face. "Just the one sister now. Stay with her, help each other. There are more children than you know. But they hide in fear and confusion. Find them and our people, find the other gods."

Adie and Tala said nothing.

They sat, frozen in the brightening light, and witnessed the death of a god and a father, of a race that had been twisted and warped for humanity's own gains.

A member of my race.

The thought washed over Adie, too large for her to truly grasp.

Adie had stopped crying. She couldn't cry anymore.

Breathing had never been so easy. Only rubble remained of the wall in her mind and the air flowed through her, crisp and fresh.

"You and Diana are part of a group, a group of the children?"

"We were. We broke away from The Children years ago. They were too scared to stop the abuse. Too scared of what powers they might be capable of wielding. Some we know are too scared to discover they haven't enough god in them to wield anything."

"How did you know? That my father was here?"

"He called to us and we told The Children. A year ago. We were sick of sitting back and doing nothing."

"What happened to Billie?"

"I killed her." Tala pulled Billie's bloody torch out from one of her pockets and laid it on the ground beside her.

Adie nodded.

"I don't expect that to endear me to you. But I'm on my own now, and I plan to keep searching for our people, our race."

"Our race." Adie's smile widened. Just moments ago, she wondered if she would ever be able to smile again.

"It's your race, whether you want it or not."

"I can still feel Mr Kenjins. And if I focus, I can hear him screaming."

"He deserves it."

"He deserved worse," Adie agreed. "But that doesn't mean I wanted this, or that I'm okay with it."

"And maybe that is why we won. I don't have the humanity, the mercy you have."

"Maybe you just need to be reminded of your human side as well?"

"Maybe. If I had someone to show me."

Adie threaded her fingers with Tala's.

She could only imagine what she looked like. Hair wild, skin dirt-smeared and eyes so black she could sleep for a week, perhaps more.

"So, what next?" Adie asked.

"We find our race, and we kill any arsehole who gets in the way."

"Okay, sure." Adie nodded and then smiled, "but maybe we can find a town that has a hotel room with a hot bath and some food first?"

Tala laughed and nodded.

They turned away from the town that continued to burn and fall into the emptiness below. Buildings collapsed and lives were taken.

Hell had finally claimed OpenFields.

About the Author

Neen Cohen is an Australian Lesbian Speculative Fiction author, and lives in Brisbane with her partner, son and fur babies. She has a Bachelor of Creative Industries from Queensland University of Technology and is a member of the Springfield Writer's Group. She's had a multitude of 'day jobs' to pay the bills but her heart has always been in the art of marking dead trees with squiggles of ink and graphite.

When she's not running after her son, spending time with her partner or working at the current 'day job', she can often be found writing while sitting against a tombstone or tree in any number of graveyards. She's also discovered a newfound passion for throwing sharp objects at thick pieces of wood (knife throwing and axe throwing) and tries to squeeze at least 30 hours into each day because sleep is for the weak.

To keep up to date with all of Neen's misadventures you can find all her links in one convenient location:

https://linktr.ee/neencohen

More from Breaking Rules Europe

- o Face of Fear by C. Marry Hultman
  978-91-986710-0-1

- o Dawson Junior G3 by Brian Wagstaff
  978-91-986710-4-9

- o New Life Cottage by Esther Jacoby
  978-91-986710-5-6

- o Liebe ist Warten by Esther Jacoby
  978-91-986710-7-0

- o Musing on Death & Dying by Esther Jacoby
  978-91-986710-6-3

- o Earth Door by Cye Thomas
  978-91-986710-2-5

- o Graffiti Stories by Nick Gerrard
  978-91-986710-1-8

- o Punk Novelette by Nick Gerrard
  978-91-986710-8-7

- o Struggle and Strife by Nick Gerrard

  978-91-9868-40-4-9

- Murder Planet by Adam Carpenter
  978-91-986710-3-2
- Generation Ship by Adam Carpenter
  978-91-9868-40-6-3
- Lost Lore and Legends – anthology
    - Paperback: 9789198671094
    - Hardcover: 9789198684100

Find us at: www.breakingrulespublishingeuro.com

CPSIA information can be obtained
at www.ICGtesting.com
Printed in the USA
LVHW090006160821
695373LV00006B/917